I0669493

The Devil Never Asks

by

Edward S. Baker

Bartholomew Jones Series

This is a work of fiction. Names, characters, places, and incidents are either the product of the author's imagination or are used fictitiously, and any resemblance to actual persons living or dead, business establishments, events, or locales, is entirely coincidental.

The Devil Never Asks

COPYRIGHT © 2022 by Edward S. Baker

All rights reserved. No part of this book may be used or reproduced in any manner whatsoever without written permission of the author or The Wild Rose Press, Inc. except in the case of brief quotations embodied in critical articles or reviews.
Contact Information: info@thewildrosepress.com

Cover Art by *Tina Lynn Stout*

The Wild Rose Press, Inc.
PO Box 708
Adams Basin, NY 14410-0708
Visit us at www.thewildrosepress.com

Publishing History
First Edition, 2023
Trade Paperback ISBN 978-1-5092-4643-4
Digital ISBN 978-1-5092-4644-1

Bartholomew Jones Series
Published in the United States of America

"Were you there when BabyX was born?" I asked.

The judge shook his head. "I didn't know there was a BabyX until right now. I'm shocked and mortified. How's my wife going to take this? To what end will the press go to embarrass my family and humiliate me? For God's sake, I'm running for the State Supreme Court of Appeals. The election is in just a few weeks."

"We know," Agent Casola said. "That's why we asked to meet you here. You should probably hire an attorney and prepare your wife for the worst. We don't know where this is going at the moment, but there's the distinct possibility of a murder charge against you, your high school FF, or both of you."

"I assure you on my word of honor as a representative of the West Virginia legal justice system that the DNA analysis may have found me guilty of fathering that poor child, but I had no knowledge of his existence until today, and most certainly I didn't murder him."

After the judge left, Special Agent Maxwell asked, "Do you believe him?"

"It's hard not to," I said.

"He's probably a liar," Agent Casola sneered. "All men are."

Praise for Edward S. Baker

Author of four science fiction novels, Edward Baker ventures into the world of contemporary crime fiction with the same zest for weaving possibility into reality. The Devil Never Asks leaves the reader with second thoughts about participating in any commercial DNA analysis programs.

Dedication

I dedicate this novel to all the victims of dead-file homicide cases, in hopes that DNA analyses eventually will bring their murderers to justice and enable their spirits to find peace.

Chapter 1

Armando Lambrucci swung the yellow bucket of his mid-sized Komatsu excavator into the porch overhang of the house on Spencer Street. The overhang cracked and fell at a forty-five-degree angle onto the decking below. Then he swung the bucket a second time, breaking the overhang into two pieces. He maneuvered the bucket under both pieces and deposited them, one at a time, into the back of a green ten-ton dump truck that sat on the street parallel to the sidewalk.

Armando liked demolition. He loved tearing into old structures that had outlived their usefulness and removing them so new ones, often buildings or homes, could be erected that would provide shelter for families or jobs for workers, or both. The demolition of the Spencer Street house took less than a day. When the house was gone, the street resembled a smile with a missing tooth, a gaping hole that hinted at the decay beneath the surface of the neighborhood. Even the cinderblocks that once had carried the load of the home's exterior walls had been removed. Armando made quick work of such demolition, and he always left the empty property immaculate.

A week later, and once all the proper permits had been issued, Armando met with the building contractor at the hole in the ground because a new four-story building was going to be erected at the Spencer Street site. Its basement would house all the electrical and heating systems, so the hole needed to be a few feet wider and at least six feet deeper.

Armando pulled his excavator close to the edge of the hole where the old basement had been and began the necessary excavation. He decided "deeper" should happen before "wider," so he began at the front left corner and proceeded toward the right. He was halfway across the front when a white ball tumbled from a plastic bag into the bed of the dump truck. He shut down his motor and shouted for assistance. Juan Baez, a general laborer, hustled over to see what he wanted.

"Hey, climb into the bed of Big Bess and see what was in that plastic bag, would ya? Might have been money."

Juan jumped onto the dump truck's running board and then worked his way to the iron stepladder which was welded onto the sidewalls. He hopped over the lip of the sidewall and found the bag almost instantly. "Mother of God," he whispered, making the sign of the cross. He leaned over the edge and shouted down to Armando.

"We got a dead one."

"What? A dead what?"

"A body. A person. A bambino."

Armand shielded his eyes from the sun with his forearm. "All three?"

"No, you moron. You got somebody dead up here. You dug up a kid's skeleton."

"Oh, shit."

Armando knew he needed to call the cops. He also knew he needed to call the general contractor, who would not be happy he had called the cops because the investigation would shut down the construction project for weeks, if not months. If he just would have buried the skeleton under another load of dirt and stone, nobody would ever have known. That would have pleased the contractor. But Armando knew if he did that, he would not be able to sleep at night. Maybe somebody killed a kid, and he did not want to be complicit by hiding the murder.

Armando called the Willow Falls Police Department. The officer who answered the phone asked if the skeleton showed evidence of foul play. It was a stupid question and one that only a forensic pathologist could answer. "How would I know?"

"Well, did you look at it?"

"Hell, no. It fell out of my excavator bucket into the back of a dump truck. I sent a kid up to see it. It shook him up so bad that he went home."

"Who owns the property?"

"Cabrillo Construction."

"That new company? Who owned it before them?"

"How would I know? I think the property has been abandoned for more than thirty years. You gotta talk with the big honcho. I'm just a heavy equipment operator."

"Okay. I'll send somebody. You know, this will probably be another dead person we can't identify. Between the homeless and the runaway druggies, we got too many unidentified cadavers to deal with. Wait there, but it'll be a while."

"How long?"

"How would I know? I'm just an electronic equipment operator."

Armando caught the humor in the response, but he did not like what he heard. He walked across the street and then down to the corner, where he bought a cup of coffee and a sweet roll at Verrigni's Quick Sack. Then he walked back to Spencer Street and sat down on the curb to wait.

Forty-five minutes later a black and tan police cruiser pulled up and three officers climbed out. "Are you the guy who found the skeleton?" asked a tall officer whose name tag identified him as "Dominici."

"Yeah, I guess I am."

"Well, *are* you, or aren't you?"

"I said 'yeah.'"

"You also said you 'guessed.' So, where was it?"

Armando nodded his head in the direction of his work. "It was down in that hole. Used to be a basement. Dirt floor."

"Who owned the house?

"Like I told the lady on the phone, how would I know? I'm just the heavy equipment operator."

"Well, if you knew, it would save us a lot of work. This is gonna be a pain in the ass."

"Show us the bones," said the black female officer. The name on her ID Tag was something Armando could not pronounce.

Armando pointed at the dump truck. "You'll have to climb up into Big Bess."

"You said they were baby bones?"

"I didn't see them. The guy who saw them said they were a baby's bones. They were in a plastic bag."

"So, you aren't the guy who found the bones?" Officer Dominici asked.

"Look, I saw a white ball fall out of a plastic bag

4

when I dumped a bucket into Big Bess."

"Big Bess is the truck, right? She isn't somebody we gotta interview?"

Armando could feel his frustration with the circular line of questioning. "Yes, Big Bess is the truck. And, no, you don't have to interview the damn truck."

Dominici looked at the other officers. "We got a funny guy here."

The female officer pointed at Dominici. "We gotta call Forensics to sift the dirt. I ain't gonna do it."

"Yeah, you're right," Dominici said. He turned to the third officer, a skinny man who appeared to be all legs. "Go call it in, Wallace."

Officer Wallace walked back to the squad car and got on the radio. Then, as he walked back to Domenici on the uneven red dirt, he adjusted his black gun belt. "They'll be here in twenty minutes."

Armando raised his hands toward the sky. "Thank God for small favors."

"You gotta problem?" Dominici asked.

"No. I'd just like to get home at a reasonable hour."

"Good. Give Wallace your name and contact information and you can go home after Forensics says they got it under control. You gotta leave your rigs here overnight, both the backhoe and the dump truck."

"It's an excavator."

"Whatever."

Chapter 2

I was named after Saint Bartholomew, one of the twelve apostles of Christ, but I am not necessarily a believer. As a police detective, I have seen enough misery and evil in the world to question if the earth's inhabitants are really the product of a good and loving creator or a spiteful and vengeful prankster. The yellow plastic bag and bones on the stainless steel table in the medical examiner's playroom led me to believe the latter.

"It's a kid, probably dead at or near birth, Detective Jones," Dr. Foster said. He was a short man, no taller than five feet four, with bushy eyebrows and pink-lensed eyeglasses. Back when I was in high school, I never would have given a guy like him a minute of my time, but here he was, fully educated as an adult and a lot more educated than I am. So, I paid attention to what he was about to say.

He stepped onto an elevated platform that compensated for his vertical challenges and waved his hand back and forth over the skeleton. "The dust and crap is the decomposed placenta and umbilical cord. The cord was never severed."

"Male or female?"

Dr. Foster pointed at the skeleton's rib cage. "Count the ribs and you'll see there are twelve pairs. A female has thirteen pairs. So, this is definitely male."

I nodded. "Got any idea about when it might have happened?"

The doctor removed his glasses and rubbed his eyes. "It's hard to say. Maybe twenty-five years ago. Maybe sooner. But the skeleton's been buried at least fifteen years. I'll need to send a piece of the skull to the university to get a good estimate."

"Cause of death?"

Dr. Foster shrugged his shoulders. "No clue. Maybe died invitro. Maybe exposure to cold air immediately after birth. Maybe strangulation. Maybe suffocation in that damn bag. Your guess is as good as mine at this point."

I could see the dead end of this investigation hurtling at me like a brick falling from a forty-story building. "How the hell am I gonna find the next of kin when the baby never saw the inside of a hospital?"

The doctor wiped his glasses with a piece of microfiber cloth and then put them back on. "Maybe DNA? I'll send some stuff out to the FBI for analysis. May take a couple of months to get an ID on possible relatives. That's the best I can do to help you."

"Thanks, Doc. I appreciate any help on this case."

Back in my office, I created a list of things to do, beginning with visits to neighbors who lived near the hole in the ground that used to be the Spencer Street house. I checked the aerial map of the city and saw that the house's backyard abutted a cemetery. "Figures," I mumbled. "The little guy was buried close to an appropriate place, but the grave digger missed the mark by fifty yards."

After my coffee break, I drove to Spencer Street and began knocking on doors. Most of the neighboring houses were occupied by new residents who, for the most part, were new Americans. They had found their way to Willow Falls from British Guiana via a short stop in the Bronx. Their homes were freshly painted in the bright colors of the tropics, and their yards were immaculate, but most spoke broken English at best. After interviewing two neighbors, I was certain this was a dead end. Nobody in the neighborhood had lived there for more than a few years.

Next, I searched home sales records at the County Clerk's Office, tracing the sales and previous owners of all Spencer Street homes for the past fifty years. The list of people to call was now longer, but information on the demolished house was sparse. It had been sold to an elderly couple in the nineteen fifties, but then sat empty after they were found dead inside from an apparent suicide pact. They had left no wills, and nobody came forward as relatives, so the house had been sitting vacant for more than fifty years before the City sold it to Cabrillo Construction for one dollar and a commitment from the company that it would build a taxable structure on the property within twelve months.

Disheartened, I abandoned the search for the identity of BabyX until the DNA analysis arrived three months later. When it did, I opened the envelope, hoping the Feds had good news for me. According to FBI analysts, the DNA sample their lab received was good, fundamentally from Anglo-Saxon forebears with ten percent Germanic and five percent Jewish ancestry. Cross-checking of DNA records from popular commercial vendors had identified possible third and fourth cousins, but that was as close as the analysts could come to an absolute identity. I filed the report in a folder containing pics of BabyX's bones, shut the file cabinet, and mentally wrote it off so I could pursue other cases.

Chapter 3

Audrey called when Michael was giving instructions to his legal assistants. He waved them out of his office so his conversation with his wife would remain private.

"Charlotte's coming home for dinner tonight," she said.

Michael stood, removed his brown suit coat, and took a sip of cold coffee from a white mug with JUDGED TO BE THE GREATEST printed on its side in royal blue ink. "Oh, good. Is she bringing Peter?"

"No, she wants to talk."

Michael wondered why Audrey had not pried more information out of Charlotte. Weren't mothers good at that sort of thing? He sat back down in his high-back leather chair. "God, I hope she isn't pregnant or anything. She's only a freshman in college. Do you think they're breaking up? Some kids do that right before a wedding. They realize maybe they love each other but not enough for a lifetime commitment."

Through the receiver, he heard a ping from their home security system as Audrey opened their front door. She was checking the mail while she spoke with him. "Let's hope not," she said as she thumbed through the envelopes and flyers. "The 'Save the Date' cards have already gone out to a hundred people."

"So, do you need me to pick up anything on the way home?"

He heard the front door close. "Yes…dinner," Audrey said. Her voice sounded disconnected from her thoughts as she inspected a flyer from her favorite women's clothing store. "I ordered it from Four Seasons, and it'll be ready at five o'clock. Put it on a credit card."

"Will do. What did you get us?"

"Shrimp Marinara and Chicken Parm for four and a tossed salad with Italian dressing."

Italian food was Michael's favorite, though West Virginia's Italian was not as good as the Italian food he remembered from his childhood in New York. "Good, there'll be enough for dinner tomorrow night, too."

"That's the idea." Audrey always liked to order more food than she and Michael could eat at a single meal. Leftovers could be re-heated in the microwave the next day and she would not have to cook.

"Okay, I'll be home at five-fifteen with the goods. What time are we expecting Charlotte?"

"Five."

"Okay. See you then."

Michael left the courthouse at four-thirty, telling his secretary to forward only important calls to his cell phone. All other business should wait until tomorrow.

He had been a county court judge for only two years, and he normally did not hear cases after four because he needed to study the laws pertaining to the next day's hearings before going home. This night was no exception, but with Charlotte's visit tonight, he decided he would go into work early the next morning to catch up on his research.

When he arrived home, Charlotte's little green Miata was in the driveway, its top down as though there were no chance of rain. He tapped the garage door opener and drove alongside her car and into his usual space in the garage.

"Hey, Pop," Charlotte said, giving him a hug and a peck on the cheek when he came into the kitchen through the door to the garage. Her amber hair was pulled back into a ponytail, and she wore a green jogging suit with a yellow stripe down the sides of each arm and leg. Her breath smelled of alcohol, and she was still two years too young to drink it legally.

Michael plopped the bag of Italian food on the kitchen counter and then kissed Audrey. She presented him with a glass of merlot.

"You are the *best*." He closed his eyes and took a sip, then turned to Charlotte. "So, what's the news, or do you want to wait to chat over dinner?"

Charlotte shrugged her shoulders. "Now's good." She took a sip from the jelly glass of wine her mother had given her before Michael had arrived home. "It's like this: Peter and I have been discussing how many kids we want to have after we get married this summer. He wants at least three and maybe four. You guys stopped at two…I'm guessing because of Charlie."

"Yes," Audrey said. "One child with Niemann-Pick's disease is enough for any family. Frankly, although we all loved your brother…God bless his soul…we were afraid to risk having another child with Childhood Alzheimer's. You know he was a handful, especially in the last year before his passing."

"That's why I'm here, Mom." Charlotte retrieved two small boxes from the big pockets of the yellow windbreaker she had hung on the back of a kitchen stool. "I bought these, and I'm hoping you'll both agree to take the test."

Michael raised an eyebrow. "What kind of test is it?"

"It's a DNA test, one that gives you your heritage, but also identifies if you carry any markers for retardation, cancer, and other syndromes."

Audrey rolled her eyes and threw her hands into the air. "Is this really necessary?"

"Yeah, I think it is. I want a large family, too, but what if I carry a marker for one of those conditions? Then I might decide not to have *any* children."

Michael cocked his head judgmentally. "And then Peter wouldn't marry you?"

Charlotte raised both palms, pleading for her parents to understand. "No, Pop. It's not like that. We might adopt or something, but I don't want to risk pregnancy if I'm carrying a marker."

"So, *you* should take the test," Audrey said. She finished her glass of wine. Then, she poured herself another and topped off Michael's glass.

"Yeah, I plan to do that, but if you both take the test…"

"Then you'll know which one of us is to blame for Charlie's condition," Audrey snapped.

Charlotte sighed and dropped her arms. "I was afraid you'd take it that way. It isn't that at all. But, in today's world I think any information we can gain is good information for the future. Like, what if his condition was something that skips generations? Then his condition wasn't *your* fault, it was passed down to you by your grandparents. See what I mean?"

"It all sounds so innocent, a simple test with no ramifications. But the Devil never asks, Charlotte. He presents you with something innocuous, like an apple, and because it looks delicious you eat it without thinking, and suddenly paradise is lost, and you pay for your sin the rest of your life."

"Jesus, Ma, give me a break. I'm just trying to use science to protect my future."

Michael interrupted the potential argument between Charlotte and Audrey. "So, you're afraid Charlie's condition might rear its ugly head in either your own children or your grandchildren?"

"I'm not *afraid*. It's just that we have access to potentially important information simply by taking a test, so why shouldn't we learn what we can? To me, it only makes sense."

Michael looked at Audrey and nodded. "I guess it's not far from the information we gained from a simple test in our day."

Audrey glared at him, upset he was not siding immediately with her position.

He turned to his daughter. "We chose to learn that you were a little girl, rather than wait to see what you were when you popped out of your mom. It was a simple test."

Charlotte smiled and nodded. "Yes. And this simple test only requires you to spit into a test tube. A few weeks later, you'll get a printout of your heritage and your disease proclivities. What you do with the information is up to you."

Audrey folded her arms across her chest, and her face took on a look of serious disapproval. "Or in the future, it'll be up to the government. They'll forbid you from having children because you're the wrong color or religion, or they'll deny you health insurance because you have a thirty percent chance of contracting cancer. I don't like it."

"So, you won't take the test, Mom?"

"Nope. Take mine back to the drug store and get your money back."

Charlotte's face showed her frustration. "What about you, Pop?"

Michael looked at Audrey, who was still scowling, and then back at Charlotte. "What harm can it do? If it means that much to you, I'll do it. But I think you'll get all the information you need from your own test. Be sure Peter takes it, too. Thus far, his family shows no signs of possible hereditary conditions, but you never know what's hiding in their genes…and it can't hurt."

Chapter 4

Michael was in his chambers when two gentlemen representing West Virginia's Conservative Party arrived for the appointment they had made the week before. His two legal assistants rose from the sofa with notes about their assignments scrawled on white legal pads. "Thanks, ladies," he said to them as they left the room. Two older gentlemen at the doorway stood aside as the young women squeezed by them.

Michael pointed to the wine-colored leather couch traditionally found in attorneys' offices. "Come in, gentlemen. The sofa has been warmed for you." He shook hands with each man. "It's good to see you, Ben. You, too, Carl. Are you guys looking forward to the return of golf season as much as I am?"

They all laughed and nodded.

"We're here on Party business, Michael." Ben tugged on the bottom of his yellow and blue striped tie. His white hair contrasted artistically with his navy-blue wool suit.

Michael suspected his visitors were meeting with him to urge leniency on the accused party in an upcoming case. "I'm not hearing a case involving one of our own, am I?"

"No, nothing so dull." Carl smiled. His appearance always looked out of character for a party leader. His brown suit needed pressing, his shoes were scuffed, and he was not wearing a tie.

"It's like this," Ben continued. "There's word Penelope Sutch is going to retire from the State Supreme Court of Appeals, and she's only into year eight out of twelve."

Michael nodded. "I heard that this morning. Any idea when?"

"She's supposed to submit her formal letter of retirement by the end of the week."

"That leaves us with a problem, Mikey," Carl said, talking down to Michael like a big brother might speak to his little brother. "We can't let the Liberals or the Republicans take her seat on the State Supreme Court of Appeals. If we can get a well-respected Conservative into her position, this State can enjoy years of the right types of decisions from the bench. No more of this liberal hooey from the likes of her and the moderate Republicans."

"How about Christine Massullo?" Michael suggested earnestly. "She's got fifteen years of bench experience and has seen it all. Her decisions are almost all right along the Party line, and we'd be replacing a woman with a woman, so there'd be no cries of gender imbalance."

"She wouldn't be bad," Ben nodded, "except her husband scored two DWIs this past year and maybe has a mistress in the wings. The other parties would kill her on her husband's indiscretions alone."

Michael shook his head. "Too bad. I really like her stance on late term abortion."

"Let's get to the point. Ben here thinks you're the candidate we need," Carl said, uncrossing his legs. "You've led a clean life, and everyone likes your wife because she's sort of a combination of Jackie Kennedy and Laura Bush"

"Yeah," Ben blurted, "she'd look real nice standing next to you on the campaign podium. You'd be the picture-perfect couple. And with her looks, she'd swing enough votes your way to counter any votes from people who only vote for old men. You couldn't lose."

Michael considered what they said for a moment. "I'm kind of young for such a giant leap. I probably need another five years of experience. Besides, I only moved to West Virginia twenty-two years ago, when I came here to go to college. I'm not what you'd call a 'native son.'"

Carl smacked his hand on the edge of Michael's desk. "All you need is enough votes and you're in like Flint, Mikey. We think you can pull it off if we get you a few key endorsements and some carefully crafted talking points. We've got people to help with all that."

Michael gave Carl a serious look. "So, who would I be indebted to? You know I can't stand the thought of political reciprocity. It's unethical."

Carl raised his left palm. "All we want is no liberal bullshit redefining the West Virginia State Constitution." He pointed at Michael's chest. "Your job is to judge the merits of every case against the laws of the land, not to create new laws from the bench the way Penelope has. With her leadership the Court has sidestepped the law-making authority of the State Legislature. Frankly, from our posture, her bench has been un-American."

Michael was silent for what felt like a full minute. "I'll talk to my wife this weekend and get back to you early next week. I'm not sure how she'll feel about campaigning, especially the way today's press snoops into a candidate's past and divulges things better left buried."

"You got anything to hide?" Ben asked.

"No. We've got a daughter who's getting married at nineteen, against my better judgment. More important, however, is that Audrey has never quite gotten over the death of our son, Charlie. If I become a candidate, every time some damn reporter adds it to an article, she'll have to relive the pain. I'm not sure I want to put her through that."

"If you don't mind my asking, how'd he die?" Carl asked.

"He died in our pool when he was twelve. At first, the police accused us of parental neglect. But we weren't home at the time, and his babysitter was on the phone with her boyfriend. We were angry, and Audrey blamed the babysitter...she was only sixteen. But the coroner discovered Charlie had suffered a myocardial infarction and was dead instantly. It wouldn't have made any difference where he was when it happened. It simply killed him on the spot. Even though he was in the pool when it happened, there wasn't any water in his lungs."

"Our staff can spin that," Ben said.

"There's nothing to spin. It was a family tragedy and we've forgiven the babysitter. In fact, we dedicated a small scholarship in Charlie's name at Marshall University, and she was its first recipient."

"It's a darn good human-interest story." Carl patted his knee. "Nobody is ever going to drag you through the mud on that one."

"Well, if you don't mind, I still want to chat with

Audrey before I give you the go-ahead to announce my candidacy."

"That's good enough for me, Michael," Ben said.

"Yeah, Mikey." Carl grasped Michael's hand and shook it vigorously. "Glad to have you on board."

Chapter 5

When her Smartphone rang, the last person Margo had expected to see on the caller ID was her stepdaughter, Raina. Just completing her freshman year at SUNY Plattsburgh in upstate New York, Raina had not ventured home since the semester break, preferring to enjoy her Spring Break partying in Myrtle Beach with a group of her Lady Cardinals' rugby teammates.

"Hey, stranger," Margo said. "To what do I owe this unexpected call from a familiar voice in a distant place?"

When she was only eighteen months old, Raina had lost her birth mom in a horrific automobile accident. The rescue squad said it was a miracle Raina had not been killed or injured, too, but secured in an infant car seat which was strapped down in the back seat, her little body was somehow spared.

"Hi, Ma. Thought I'd give you a buzz. Classes end this Friday and exams follow right afterward."

Margo could picture Raina's arrival in a car filled to the brim with books, dirty clothes, and computer and sports equipment. "Are you warning me to hurry up finishing my laundry, so I can begin yours when you get home?"

"Nope. I'm calling to ask if you'd mind if I come back up to Plattsburgh in July. Coach is looking for a few girls to assist with the summer youth rugby camp.

It's girls only and it's a paid position. So, can I?"

Margo was not sure how this plan would fly with Henry. "I know Dad is hoping you'll spend some time at home this summer, but I'm sure he won't mind, as long as you'll be home for June and August. Is it good pay?"

"Not as much as I'd earn if I did fulltime work at the supermarket. But it's a privilege to be asked to be an assistant. There's something else…I'll be home only part of August, Ma…just the first two weeks, and then I'm back at practice with the team. We have a good chance of winning the State's this year, you know."

Margo smiled. "I know honey. We're so proud of you. So, will we see you as soon as you're finished with your finals?"

"Yeah, Ma. Gotta go. Give my love to Dad. Bye."

Raina hung up abruptly, as she always did when she had something more important on her agenda, such as telling her coach she had permission to work at his summer rugby camp.

When Henry came home, Margo gave him a big kiss. "How did classes go today, Mr. Lumpas?"

He plopped his distressed leather briefcase on a kitchen stool, then loosened the solid blue tie that lay over his gray madras shirt and unbuttoned his collar. "Actually, it went better than I thought it would. Only two girls vomited when we dissected the cats."

"That's horrible. Did you have to clean it up?"

"Nope, it's maintenance's job. I just called the principal's office and asked them to send the 'barf bandito.' Mr. DeAngelo arrived quickly, mopped it up, and sprayed the lab with air freshener."

"That was good of him." Margo said, rinsing a

dirty washcloth in the sink. She really didn't care about the details of Henry's work, but when he came home from work every afternoon, she tried to let him debrief as if his world was all important.

"Yeah. I'm glad I don't have his job, but he's our hero. The entire high school depends on him to save the day. I mean, on an average day at least three kids drop their lunch trays onto the cafeteria floor before they take a bite of food. DeAngelo just brings his mop and bucket and waits in the corner of the cafeteria for each day's klutzes to do their thing."

Henry looked around the kitchen. "Kids home yet?"

"No. Zoe is at the high school orientation program."

"Oh, yeah, I forgot about that." He opened the refrigerator and retrieved a can of diet cola. "She seems extraordinarily excited about leaving middle school, doesn't she?"

"She's excited about playing interscholastic soccer…and maybe about dating. Remember, you told her she couldn't date until she's sixteen."

"I also can't believe she's making noise about wanting to follow me into teaching…and Biology, at that. Of course, her career plans will likely change once she hits high school."

"You're a good role model for her…and all the kids. They're lucky to have you as a father. And then, why wouldn't she want to be a teacher? The pay isn't bad, and the benefits are superlative."

"Where's little Louie?"

"He's over at Joey's playing video games. Joey got the latest Star Wars game for his birthday."

Henry wasn't happy about Louie's interest in video games. "I suppose Louie's gonna want the same thing."

Margo shrugged a "yes, I guess," with her shoulders and changed the subject. "Raina called earlier."

"When is she due home?"

"They're going into exams now, so it won't be too long. She's been invited to coach at Plattsburgh's kids' summer camp in July. She'll give you all the details when she gets home, but I think we'll see her only in the beginning of the summer and then maybe a week before she goes back for Fall practice."

"Nice opportunity for her." Henry sighed. "But not so good for us. As much as we may not like it, we've got to let her go out on her own now, don't we? It's the nature of things that she finds her own way, makes her own life."

Margo nodded. "You're a good father, Henry."

Henry opened his briefcase and pulled out four cellophane-wrapped boxes. "I finally got these today."

"The DNA kits?"

Over the past few months Henry had been excited about the possibility of developing a biology course module about DNA. He was especially interested in how DNA had been used by top scientists to trace the movement of Homo sapiens from Africa into Europe and Asia.

"Yeah. If we can get them done before the end of the school year, I can plan the DNA unit for next Fall's classes. It'll be interesting to see how our DNA is transferred to our kids, and in what proportions. I'm expecting each kid to be a little different from their siblings."

"Don't the major educational publishing houses offer DNA units?"

"Yeah, but they're all canned and lack good 'discovery' content." He raised his pointer finger into the air. "I think it'll be better if my students see real analytical reports and then discover principles of genetics emerging from the samples of their own DNA."

Margo did not like being lectured to, so she lectured back. "Still, some of your kids come from homes where their fathers are unknown, even by their mothers. Are you sure you want to open that can of worms?"

"Mrs. McAndrews, the school psychologist, is going to help those students whose DNA analyses identify uncomfortable attributes. I mean, this Fall's will be a first run and it's only an experiment. Besides, all the parents must sign an approval form before their kids participate in this assignment. I think we've covered most of the bases."

"You didn't bring a kit for Raina," Margo noted.

"It's not so important for my project. Besides, her genetics don't flow from your family. I wish they did." Henry finally opened his can of cola and took a sip. "Because she has a different birth mother, I think including her genetics would only present apples and oranges to my students."

Before dinner that evening, Henry, Margo, Zoe, and Louie all opened their DNA kits and filled the small test tubes with saliva. "Thanks to all of you for helping me develop this new unit for my biology courses." Henry smiled at his wife and children. "This is going to herald a new adventure for our family,"

Margo and Zoe rose from the table and went into the kitchen. When they returned, Zoe was carrying a dish of green beans and a small bowl of mashed potatoes. And Margo was carrying a large platter of her culinary specialty, baby back ribs.

After dinner, Zoe and Louie cleaned the dishes while Margo dressed in a brown pants suit and opened the front door of their Cape Cod home.

"Going to Mimi's?" Henry asked.

"No, silly. It's Thursday. I need to play the organ for choir practice. Besides, it's best I run through the hymns a few times before church on Sunday. Nothing's more embarrassing than hitting a bad note when the congregation is singing."

Chapter 6

Margo was hosting her card group's monthly pinochle game when the postman lifted the squeaky lid on her mail slot and all the letters and business flyers came tumbling onto the foyer floor.

"I feel like one of Pavlov's dogs," she said as she excused herself from her table of four. "Every time the mail slot squeaks, I just have to go clean up the floor. It's terrible, isn't it?"

"You should get Henry to oil that lid," Linda Lunsford said. "My Chet wouldn't tolerate that sort of thing."

Margo quickly walked to the foyer, brushed the assorted letters into a pile, and plopped them onto a small table which stood against the wall near the stairs to the second-floor bedrooms.

"Can I get anybody more wine?" she asked as she returned to the family room.

Her three friends all shook their heads.

"Isn't your anniversary sometime soon?" Penelope Higgins asked, adjusting the half-glasses which perched on the tip of her pointed nose.

"Yes, next week." Margo sat back down at the card table.

"Is it really?" Linda asked. "How long have you two been married?"

Margo cut the deck of cards that Linda had slid to

her. "This Wednesday will be fourteen years."

"I thought you have a daughter in college." Linda pulled the deck of cards back to her place on the table and began to deal. "Is she a genius or something?"

"That's Henry's daughter by his first marriage," Penelope said. "His wife died in a car accident, the poor dear. I was in high school, but I remember the television coverage. Wasn't she drunk or something?"

Margo cleared her throat. She hated explaining her personal life to people who have no business knowing about it. "The other driver was drunk and had a revoked license. Henry was left a single parent in the blink of an eye, and Raina was only eighteen months old."

"How did he ever manage?" Loretta Robertson asked. "Men just aren't programmed for raising kids, cleaning house, and keeping down a fulltime job."

"That's how he met you, isn't it, Margo?" Penelope said. It seemed like Penelope knew as much about Margo's life as Margo did.

"Yes," Margo replied. "I was in college and needed a job. Henry needed childcare assistance, so I cared for Raina all day, and when Henry came home from work, I went to classes."

"That must have been hard for you," Loretta said.

"It wasn't too bad. Raina was just a toddler, and whenever she took a nap, I studied…well, unless I decided to help Henry out a bit with his laundry or cleaning."

"I'll bet you helped him out with more than that," Penelope said, spreading her handful of cards into a fan and beginning to sort them. "He married you, didn't he?"

The ladies all giggled.

"That didn't come until much later, girls. I was only nineteen when I came to work for him, and we didn't get married until I was twenty-four."

"Didn't you have to get married?" Penelope asked, peeking over her hand of cards.

"Have some more to drink, Penelope, and quit making insinuations which are none of your business," Linda said. "If I recall, you did half the boys in high school until you found one who'd marry you, even if you were a whore."

"Woo hoo," Loretta cackled. "We'd better get back to cards before we get into a cat fight." Her eyes opened wide when she looked at the hand of cards she'd been dealt. "I bid twenty-six."

The girls played cards until four o'clock, and then they broke up to go home and fix dinner for their husbands. As she closed the door on the last woman to leave, Margo remembered the mail and picked through it. The one addressed to her from "DNA Masters" caught her attention. It had been six weeks since Henry had mailed the DNA tests to the manufacturer for analysis, and she knew he would be excited the results had arrived. She opened it and began to read. Her DNA described her as eighty-seven percent Scots/Irish, five percent Germanic, and eight percent Jewish.

"That's interesting," she muttered. "I didn't know we had any German blood in the family."

Then she checked the closest relatives. There was a ninety-eight percent chance she was a parent of Louis Henry Lumpas, Jr. and Zoe Lumpas, both of Marshfield, New York. There was also ninety-eight percent chance she was a parent of BabyX of Willow Falls, New York.

Margo's past rushed in on her as though someone had cast a dark veil over her life as a wife and mother in an upscale community. *How did they know I had another baby?* Suddenly she saw herself at sixteen, having casual sex with her friend Michael on a dirty mattress in an abandoned row house near the cemetery. Then she relived the pain and felt the shock and loneliness of giving birth to a stillborn child on that same mattress. Then the horror of placing her stillborn son in a plastic bag and burying him in the dirt-floor basement of an abandoned house with no funeral, no words spoken from the Bible, and no songs of farewell or salvation. She felt like the world's worst sinner.

She dug through the mail, looking for the other reports. Only Louie's had arrived today. She hurried through the mail again, double checking the origin of every letter. *Yes, just Louie's and mine.* Curling her report in her fist, she climbed the stairs and buried it beneath her underwear in the dresser drawer which she was confident Henry would never open.

A voice from downstairs startled her. "I'm home, Ma."

The front door slammed shut. It was Louie.

"I'm upstairs. I'll be right down."

Margo squeezed her fists to reduce the shaking of her hands, and took three deep breaths, forcefully pushing the air out of her lungs before she called down the stairs. "Do you have much homework, honey?"

"Just math…Ma, where'd you hide the cookies?"

"None left. Your dad finished them all last night."

Louie said something in a complaining voice, but Margo could only decipher the sentiment and not his words.

****

Zoe walked from the middle school to the high school and then rode home with her dad. When Zoe and Henry came into the kitchen together, Margo and Louie were busy double checking his math homework at the kitchen table.

"Any interesting mail?" Henry asked.

Margo didn't know why, but Henry always wanted to know what was in the mail or where it was, even though she always left it in the same place. "It's on the foyer table," she called out. *You'd think he'd open his eyes and see it where I always leave it.*

Heavy thumping on the stairs let Margo know that Zoe was heading up to her room to begin her homework. Henry came back into the kitchen opening the letter which was addressed to Louie from DNA Masters. "Did any more of these come in the mail today?"

"Any more of what?"

"The DNA reports that I've been expecting. Louie's came today."

"Oh, how nice. I didn't really look at the mail. It came while the girls were here, and I just plopped it on the table."

"What's it say, Daddy?" Louie asked.

Henry ignored his son and kept talking to his wife. "Must be they just send them as they finish them. This is great, though. Louie is eighty-five percent Anglo/Saxon, five percent Norwegian, five percent German/Austrian, three percent Lithuanian, and two percent Jewish. It's going to be interesting to see how he compares to you and me and especially to Zoe. I'm going to begin the comparison charts for my DNA module tonight. This is a good start."

Margo feigned support of Henry's project, which now threatened to expose her past. "Good. I know you're anxious to get started on your project. Hopefully, the rest of the reports will arrive soon."

"What's 'angle sextant,' Daddy?" Louie asked.

Henry kept ignoring his son. He looked perplexed. "Who's BabyX?"

Margo gulped. "Who?"

"It says here there's an eighty-six percent chance Louie has a brother named 'BabyX.' Who the heck is that?"

A shot of fear pierced Margo's gut. She got up from the kitchen table and took the report from Henry. She looked carefully at it. "This *is* odd, isn't it?" she said, pretending curiosity. "I wouldn't worry about it, though. It may just be a mistake…Besides, he's got only an eighty-six percent chance of being related."

She handed the report back to Henry, who stuffed it into his briefcase. "We'll figure it out later. Right now, I need to focus my attention on my lesson plans for tomorrow." He walked into the family room.

Margo looked at Louie, who had laid his head on his arms on top of his mathematics assignment. "I think we've done enough for tonight, sweetheart. Why don't you go outside and see if somebody wants to play."

Louie took his math worksheet and his pencil and left the kitchen. A moment later, Margo heard the front door open and slam closed.

She sat back in her chair at the dark pine kitchen table. Her face was contorted with worry as her head swirled with the details and potential risks of the coming situation. She hoped Zoe's report would not also claim a sibling relationship to BabyX, but if there was any real science behind DNA analyses, it most certainly would. What could she do about it? Nothing, except keep her own report hidden. But how long would it be before she would have to confront the truth and tell Henry she had given birth to a child before they met? She feared what such a revelation would do to their relationship. Would Henry divorce her? How could she explain BabyX to her family? It was too much to bear. She felt nauseous, so she left the kitchen, climbed the stairs, and got into her bed. And wept.

Chapter 7

I was sitting on a stool at Ruby's Red Hots, dressed in khakis and a white shirt, no tie. My elbows were on the counter, a hotdog in one hand and a napkin in the other, so I could wipe grease and meat sauce from my horseshoe moustache. Beside me sat Lt. Helen Martin, shoveling a hotdog with meat sauce and onions into her mouth. Like me, Helen was dressed in plainclothes—blue jeans and a sweatshirt—looking more like a shopper than an armed police detective. The department's only black female detective, she had developed a camaraderie with me while investigating homicides over the past three years.

Helen lifted her bun into the air. "These things are addicting, aren't they?" A trickle of grease ran down her little finger and onto her wrist. She wiped it off with a paper napkin.

"For me, absolutely. But my wife won't eat here," I said. "I brought her here when she was four months pregnant. She had one hotdog and suffered indigestion all night."

Helen laughed and wiped a plug of meat sauce off her lower lip. "She doesn't blame that hotdog for her miscarriage, does she?"

I wiped my mouth with my napkin. "No, but I think sometimes she'd like to."

"So how many cases are you investigating right

now?" Helen asked.

I sprinkled a few drops of habanero sauce onto my hotdog. "I've got nine. How about you? You close to solving Romeo and Juliette yet?"

"I've got six. Romeo and Juliette may not need solving. It looks open and shut to me. I just have to file the final report."

"So, tell me about it. I don't know much…just overheard some of the guys talking."

"It's like this: You got a guy and girl from opposite sides of the tracks. The guy is black, and the girl is Puerto Rican."

"Possibly a good match."

Helen nodded. "Well, both sets of parents don't like the relationship. Romeo's father is a doctor and the girl's father is a deadbeat. The doc tells the son to ditch the girl. The girl's mother wants her to date Puerto Rican guys—you know, keep the line pure. Got the picture?"

"Yeah, I guess." I swallowed a bite of hotdog. "They bumping uglies?"

"Probably. So, the two kids get upset and decide to show their parents they should have butted out of their personal lives."

"How'd they do that…run away together?"

"Nope. They enter a suicide pact. They sneak out at night and meet up at the high school, where they divide a bottle of prescription pain killers and swallow them all."

I am always interested in identifying the culprit. "Who gave them the prescription meds?"

"I think the boy stole them from his father's stash."

"He a dealer?"

"The father? No. He keeps a bag full of stuff to give to patients who can't afford drugs at the pharmacy."

"So, go on. This is interesting."

"Well, third shift security finds the two kids lying unconscious on the concrete patio outside of the maintenance department. They call the ambulance, and the kids get hauled off to the hospital."

"Which one died?"

"Neither. Because they divided the pills, neither one took enough to make it to the long sleep. And they got their stomachs pumped. So, Romeo comes to first, and he learns that Juliette is comatose. He figures she's successfully dead and he's a failure because he isn't. Of course, his parents are pissed and blame the whole incident on the girl's family."

I finished my hotdog and signaled to the waitress that I wanted another.

She took a pen from the breast pocket of her red and white striped apron and looked at me quizzically. "Three?"

"Yeah. The first two weren't bad. I'm hoping you can do better on the next one."

The waitress smiled. "You've been in here too often to make a crack like that. Your limit is usually two."

I turned back to Helen. "So, go on…"

"Well, the kid has been watching *Sons of Anarchy* and decides to go out like Jax."

"Motorcycle into a truck?"

"Well, sort of. What he did was climb onto a bridge railing over the crosstown and jump off in front of an oncoming semi."

"Ewww. Sounds brutal."

"Yeah. He jumped too soon, broke both legs and his pelvis when he hit the concrete highway, and then was hit and dragged a couple of hundred feet under the tires of the semi. Don't know how long he was conscious, but the driver said the kid was screaming when he hit him. Shook him up real bad."

"Shook the driver up a bit, too, I imagine."

"You're funny…"

My third hotdog arrived. I gave the waitress a five-dollar bill and told her to keep the change. "So, what about the girl?"

"Well, she finally comes out of her coma, and after ten days in the hospital learns her boyfriend bit the bullet and she's missed the funeral."

"What did she do?"

"She goes to see his parents. His mother won't let her in. Mom calls her a whore and a clap trap and tells her to get out of her family's life forever. On her way home, Juliette drives to the middle of the Okwaho Bridge during that massive ice flow two months ago and jumps into the river."

"No way she survived that."

"Nope."

"They ever find her body?"

"Yeah, down near the lock south of the city, caught on the branch of a Hemlock tree. Her body was mangled pretty bad by the icebergs."

"Sad story. No wonder you call them Romeo and Juliette."

"It gets worse."

"Really?"

"Yeah. Juliette's mother is so distraught she goes

to Romeo's home and rings the doorbell. The maid answers. Mom shoots the maid, three rounds to the chest, thinking she's Romeo's mother."

"Let me guess…the maid was black."

"You're pretty smart for a detective."

****

Back at my desk after lunch, I thought about the tragedy of Romeo and Juliette's story—how the families tried to control who the kids would love—how the kids tried to hurt their parents—how both kids lived up to their suicide pact—how race played a role in the maid's death. *There's no way you could make this stuff up.*

My desktop computer pinged, announcing a new email. This one came from the FBI, Missing Persons Tasks Force, Washington, DC. All the message said was:

Call me.
FBI Special Agent Casola
(202) 324-3000

I dialed the number and asked for Agent Casola. The operator asked for a moment to find her in the directory, and then she connected me to Casola.

The phone rang three times. "Casola here." It was a woman's voice.

"Are you Special Agent Casola?"

"That's what I said. Mona Casola here. How can I help you?"

"This is Lt. Bart Jones, Willow Falls Police Department, New York."

"Oh yeah. Thanks for returning my call…er…my email. I think I may have something for you." Rustling and ratting sounds came over the phone. She was obviously buried in paperwork. "Here it is…"

I waited, not so much anxious, but more interested in this character on the other end of the phone.

"Listen, Bart," she began, "you solved your BabyX case yet?"

"Nope. I've sort of put it on the back shelf."

"Well, maybe you need to pull it forward a bit."

"Why's that?"

"You know some woman named Margo Lumpas, a.k.a. Margo Borst?"

"Never heard of her. How do you spell both names?"

Agent Casola spelled them for me, slowly.

"So, how does she figure into this case?" I asked.

"We got a DNA update last week."

"Update?"

"Yeah. Those commercial analysis places get lots and lots of DNA every day. They run the reports, and then on a quarterly basis they update all their files. If someone gets a significant piece of new information, they're notified. So, the Bureau ordered the work up on the DNA you guys got a few months back. They updated us last week. Make sense?"

"Yeah, I'm following you."

"So, the update says this Margo woman is probably the mother of BabyX.

A shot of adrenalin ran through the skin on my back. "Really?"

"Yeah. It says ninety-eight percent probability. But it gets better. She lives one zip code away, in the Town of Marshfield. Close, right?"

"Yeah. It's right next door."

"Well, go get her, Hondo."

I wiped my forehead with my palm. "Can I get a copy of the updated report?"

"You betcha. I'll scan it and email it to you when we hang up."

"Thanks, Agent Casola. I'll send a note of appreciation to your boss."

"Your federal tax dollars at work."

Chapter 8

While I waited impatiently for my computer to ping, I opened my filing cabinet and pulled out the folder marked "BabyX." Dropped into the folder, but never opened, was an envelope from the county medical examiner. I peeled it open and read its contents. According to Dr. Foster, the State University of New York at Albany had analyzed the skull fragment and determined BabyX was no more than two days old at the time of death. His approximate date of death was September—December 1999. According to the report, if the skull fragment had been over two hundred years old, they could have been more precise, but their confidence in the suggested period of death was ninety-five percent.

Details were beginning to come together. On a hunch, I dropped by the Willow Falls City School District and spoke in confidence with the Assistant Superintendent, Dr. Elise Grogan. She was a tall woman in her fifties, wearing a green pant suit and brown flats. Her white pullover top displayed a ring of fat around her waist. Her salt and pepper hair was pulled into a ponytail, held in place by a white scrunchie.

"I'm looking for a list of all registered high school students during the 1999-2000 school year," I said.

"We say 'academic year,' Detective," Grogan told

me. "Do you want both male and female?"

"Yes, that would be good."

"Can I ask the nature of your inquiry?"

"It's an old case, possibly a murder which never should have happened and never has been solved."

Grogan went to her bookshelf. She inspected a row of leather-bound books on the second shelf from the bottom and then slid one out and blew the dust from it. "This should do, unless you want a computer print-out. The bonus with a yearbook is you get pictures to go along with the names."

"I hadn't thought of that. This is actually better than I had anticipated."

I took the 2000 Golden Eagles Yearbook from Grogan and thumbed through the color photos of seniors. Margo Borst was not among them. Then I checked the juniors. Bingo!

Although the photos were smaller, Margo Angela Borst was there, staring at me from a black and white image taken by a school photographer twenty-five years ago. She was wearing a white blouse and she was not really smiling. Her dark hair was shoulder length, falling clumsily over cheeks that whispered she was probably chunky, but not fat. Not really.

"May I borrow this book?" I asked, closing it so Grogan could not see the page that had captured my attention.

"Yes, but please bring it back in one piece. It's the only one we have in the administrative offices, though there may be another copy in the library."

"Thank you. I guess you've given me everything I need."

"Will you do me a favor, Detective?"

"What's that?"

"If you discover something that will reflect negatively upon the school district, will you call me before you tell the press? That will give me time to brief the superintendent and time for us to develop a spin which reduces the negativity. Recently, our district has been the target of much negative press and, frankly, we don't need any more."

"That's fair. You've been very helpful to me, and the least I can do is return the favor."

"Thank you, Detective."

****

"Helen?" I asked.

Helen Martin spun around in her desk chair. She looked perky today, dressed in a black pant suit, her hair freshly braided into a goddess cut. Her lips a glossy maroon. "What's up, Jonesy?"

"You going out tonight?"

"You asking?"

"Come on. I'm married, and I'm not messing around at work."

"Someplace else?"

"I only got time to mess around with my wife…and only when she's in the mood."

"I spent half a day in the beauty parlor yesterday to look like this. Figure somebody's gonna ask me out."

"Not if your breath still smells like an onion-covered hotdog." I patted a small stack of papers I held in my hand. "You got time to come with me on an interview?"

"A woman alone?"

"Yeah, probably."

"Be back by five?"

43

"Hope so. Maybe gonna arrest her."

Helen hopped up and grabbed her black faux leather purse. "As long as you do the intake paperwork, count me in."

****

Helen and I knocked on the door of a cape cod in an older section of Marshfield, an upscale town bordering Willow Falls. The house was gray with green shutters. A single car garage was attached on the right side. Its driveway consisted of two lines of concrete with a strip of grass in between.

I lived in a Willow Falls neighborhood full of single-family homes. Martin lived in a two-family in Glen Arbor, a struggling small town on the northern border of the city. Marshfield snuggled in-between Willow Falls and Glen Arbor. What made Marshfield different is most of its residents were college educated and worked in well-paying jobs in industry or government. The State capitol was less than half an hour's commute. Marshfield town cops did not have much to do except prowl the streets for kids and people who obviously did not belong and usher them back across the border into Willow Falls or neighboring suburbs.

A neighbor saw us standing on the cape's small porch. She was bowed a little from age, probably in her early eighties, and her short curly hair was gray with a tinge of blue. "They're away," she told us as if we had asked. "He works. She's probably shopping. Can I help you in some way?"

I showed her my badge. "Do these people give you any trouble?"

"Land sakes, no. They're good people. She plays

the organ at my church. He's a high school science teacher. They're very upstanding and well-respected in this neighborhood. Good kids, too. Smart."

"What time should we come back if we want to speak with them?" Helen asked.

"Did they do something wrong?'

"Nope. Nothing we know of. Just need to speak with them. Hope they can help us with information we need to solve a case we're working on."

"I suppose you should come back at dinner time. He usually gets home around six."

"Thank you, ma'am," Helen said.

As we left, I mumbled, "You gave her a mouthful of information she doesn't need to know."

"I didn't say anything about the case. She's a busybody, anyway. She's gonna tell everybody on this block we were here. It's better she should think we're just looking for information."

"There goes the sleepy little neighborhood."

"S'pose we should have touched base with the Marshfield PD before we dropped by?"

"Probably would have been the right protocol. I guess we should go there now and then I'll drop you back at the station so you can rest up for your big date tonight. Who're you going out with anyway?"

"Nobody…not since you took me out of the office where those handsome young bachelors could see how smart I look with this new 'do.'"

"Don't you know better than to pee in the pond you go swimming in?"

"Who but a cop is gonna marry a cop, especially a female cop who's already made detective? The fish in that pond is getting fewer and fewer every day."

"S'pose you're right."

****

I drove my tan Camry a mile northeast and parked outside the Marshfield Police Department, a one-story building which was long and narrow and easily could have been converted into a strip mall if, in fact, it hadn't been a strip mall which had been converted into a police department. I opened the door for Helen and then followed her inside. A lone officer sat at a desk reading a scientific magazine. His red hair and freckled skin tagged him as the descendent of a Viking or a leprechaun.

"Detectives Martin and Jones from Willow Falls PD," I announced.

"You got an emergency?" he asked.

"No, not really."

"Gotta question for you, then. This article I'm reading says humans and chimpanzees share ninety-eight percent DNA."

"So?" Helen asked. "Most of the guys I know are apes."

"You aren't from around here, are you?"

"Not Marshfield."

"It's like this: This article says chimpanzees share a bunch of bad behaviors with humans…things like rape, and war, and domination, and power drives. If we could isolate the DNA that causes chimpanzees to do bad stuff and remove it from their genes, and they turned peaceful…couldn't we do the same thing to people and eliminate most of the really bad crimes that peeps do?"

Helen looked at me. "This is beyond my pay grade. Are we in a police station or a biology class?"

"Can we pull you out of your magazine and ask you for some help with police work?" I asked.

The officer gave us a look of exasperation, stuck a piece of paper in the magazine, and plopped it face down on his desk. "How can I help you two?"

"We got a possible murder in Willow Falls, possibly perpetrated by a Marshfield resident, or possibly she knows who did it. We want to interrogate her. How do we get permission to do that?"

"A woman?"

"Yeah," Helen said.

The officer looked at Helen for a moment and then returned his eyes to me. "Best thing is to have us bring her down here and you do your interrogation by invitation from Chief Parillo".

"And if we want to arrest her?" I asked.

"We'll do it and then transfer her to you guys for formal charges and processing, assuming the deed was done in your jurisdiction. You got a warrant?"

"All we have right now is DNA evidence linking her to the deceased."

"Like I said, we'll bring her in for questioning. You do the questioning. Anything beyond that is Chief Parillo's decision."

I gave the officer Margo Borst Lumpas' name and address and asked that I be called when an interview had been set up. I did not care what time of day, but I wanted the Marshfield Police Department to get on it as soon as possible. And I wanted a female Marshfield officer in the room during the interrogation.

"That's all up to Chief Parillo."

Chapter 9

"This is Chief Parillo, Marshfield. Are you Jones?"
The chief's voice was husky over the phone. Maybe he
had a cold.

"Yup, Bartholomew Jones, Detective."

"So, what do you have?"

I spoke like the professional cop I am. "I have a
skeleton. Dead baby, probably 1999. Bones were dug
up in the basement of a house during an urban renewal
project."

"How does this involve Mrs. Lumpas?"

"Did a DNA analysis using part of the skull. Came
back she is ninety-eight percent the probable mother."

"Who did the analysis?"

"The FBI."

"Oh." The chief sounded surprised that a
competent agency had handled the task. "Was the baby
murdered?"

"We don't know. There's lots of questions
surrounding the deceased."

"You know her husband is a science teacher and
upstanding guy?"

"Yup, and she plays organ in some church."

"Yeah, my church."

"Does everybody in Marshfield go to the same
church?"

"No. We got some Muslims, Jews, and Catholics.

But she's a Baptist. So am I."

"So, you don't dance?"

"What kind of crack is that? You want to interrogate Mrs. Lumpas or not?"

"Yeah, I do. Sorry if I offended you. It comes from an old joke."

"Yeah, I heard it before." The chief paused for a moment. "All right, I got her set up to come in on Friday during the school day. She says she can be here at ten o'clock. That good for you?"

"Yup, that's fine. You're not sending a squad car to pick her up?"

"Nope. Don't want to upset the neighbors. This is a peaceful community, and we don't want to make a scene. She'll leave her home like she's going to the grocery store, drive herself in, and meet you here at ten."

"Does she know what this is about?"

"She started crying over the phone when I told her who I was."

I tucked Mrs. Lumpas' tearful response away in my head for future reference. And Helen's Friday schedule was already full. "So, she figures we've got the goods on her. Do you have a woman who can be there as a witness?"

"Just a part-timer, but she's good. That okay with you?"

I didn't care if she was full-time or part-time, as long as she could be there and vouch that I didn't harass, intimidate, or sexually assault Mrs. Lumpas during the interrogation. "Yup. Okay if I tape the interview?"

"Figured you would. You guys got portable stuff in

Willow Falls?"

"Yup. I'll bring it. Thanks, Chief. I look forward to meeting you."

Chapter 10

I reviewed my list of questions with Helen Martin, paperclipped the list to the inside of my notebook, and then drove from the Willow Falls PD to Marshfield, where I parked in a visitor's space in front of the Police Department. The sky was gray and threatened rain, and the air was cool for early September. Silently I hoped the first snow of winter would not surprise upstate New York during the first week of October as it once had, shutting down the power grid for four days.

When I reached the front door, I paused to let two senior citizens leave the building before I entered. Inside, I stood at the counter for a moment before my eyes met those of the same officer I had spoken with several days before. "Detective Jones, Willow Falls PD, here to see Chief Parillo."

The desk sergeant motioned over his shoulder with his thumb. "The room's ready for you. Want coffee?"

"Thanks, but no. Is the interviewee here yet?"

"Not unless she snuck in behind those two who just paid their parking ticket." The desk sergeant jotted a few notes on his desk pad and then looked up. "You didn't bring your sidekick with you today?"

"No, she's busy with a murder that's turned into a racial incident. You probably read about it in the Gazette."

"Saw something about it on the front page

yesterday, I think. Wacky…the way that case turned out…the maid and all."

I nodded. The paper had run the suicide pact story on the front page. And then in the middle of the three-section edition it included a long editorial about racism's role in the case. I was sure Helen Martin was up to her eyeballs in work as a result of the paper's misrepresentation of facts. But for the moment I had more pressing business. "Chief in?"

"Nope. He said to get you settled in and introduce you to Patrolman Tuttle before the interrogation begins."

"Tuttle?"

"Yeah, she's the woman we use for instances like these…when we're worried about claims of sexual harassment, especially if we're a couple of men on a woman interviewee."

"She here yet?"

"Yes, I am."

I turned and looked behind me. Patrolman Tuttle had quietly come in the front door behind me, paper coffee cup in hand. She was dressed in a Marshfield PD uniform, matching gray shirt and slacks with a navy-blue stripe down the side of the leg. Her curly blonde hair was pinned back into a bun. I thought she was pretty, which would work well in helping Margo Lumpas calm her nerves before the questions began, or if she broke down during the questioning.

I extended my hand. "Happy to meet you, Tuttle."

She shook my hand and smiled. "Chief tells me this case could be touchy." She took a bottle of hand sanitizer from her purse and cleaned her hands. "The female is married to a well-known teacher."

"Yes, apparently so. I don't know him, but it seems he's popular with the kids and their parents. The wife plays organ in the Baptist Church."

The desk sergeant interrupted us. "A car just pulled in out front. Could be your interviewee. Why don't you go discuss the case back in the staff room?"

"Come on, Detective," Tuttle said. "It's right down here."

I followed Tuttle down a narrow corridor and into a small room with no windows. A gray metal table sat in the middle of the room with two matching chairs on each side. A white water cooler sat in one corner. A small stack of paper cups lay on top of its five-gallon plastic water bottle.

We sat, Tuttle on the left and me on the right, on the side of the table facing the door. "Always face the door," I said as I pulled out my chair.

"Yeah, that's what I've heard," Tuttle replied.

The door opened, and the desk sergeant's arm pointed into the room. In walked a woman in her late thirties, wearing a conservative gray dress and black flats. Her make-up was modest. Behind her came a man in a blue pin-striped suit. He did not look like a high school biology teacher.

"Lance Freeborn," the man said. "I'm representing Mrs. Lumpas." He handed both Tuttle and me a business card.

I looked at the card. "She hasn't been charged with anything, Mr. Freeborn."

"And we don't want her charged unnecessarily. I'm here to ensure she doesn't self-incriminate in any of her responses."

I could feel my frustration rising. I had not asked a

question yet, but already I was beginning to feel this interview was going to go nowhere.

"Detective Bart Jones, Willow Falls PD," I said. "The lady to my left is Patrolman Tuttle, with Marshfield PD."

"You feeling okay, honey?" Patrolman Tuttle asked. "Would you care for some water or a cup of coffee?"

"No, I'm good," Margo replied in a soft voice. "I'm just nervous. I've never been dragged into a police station before. I've never even gotten a parking ticket."

"Then let me get started." I placed a small digital tape recorder on the table and pushed the ON button. "I'm attached to the Willow Falls Police Department. Due to the nature of a case I'm investigating, Marshfield PD has granted me permission to use these facilities to interview you. I'm hoping your responses will help me to close the book on this case."

Margo nodded, then wiped her nose with a crumpled tissue.

"Do you have any idea why I asked to speak with you this morning?"

Margo shook her head nervously. Red splotches had begun showing on her neck.

"Last spring, during an urban renewal project, an excavator uncovered the bones of a baby boy in what had been the basement of an abandoned two-story house on Spencer Street in Willow Falls. Are you familiar with Spencer Street?"

Margo looked at her attorney. He nodded. "Yes, I am," she said. "I lived a few blocks from there when I was growing up."

"The bones were examined by a forensic

pathologist, who determined the baby died within two days of birth. The State University verified the deceased child was male and he died sometime between October and December of 1999."

Margo nodded.

Her lawyer whispered something into her ear, then he turned to me. "When Mrs. Lumpas nodded, she was indicating she understands the details which you were telling her, not that she was familiar with those details or that she knew anything about the deceased male child before today."

I continued. "A sample of bone tissue was sent to the FBI forensics Unit, where it underwent DNA analysis. The results of the analysis were cross-examined against the records of all commercial DNA labs in the United States. Do you know what they determined, Mrs. Lumpas?"

Margo's eyes shifted back and forth quickly between her attorney and me. Then she shook her head.

"They determined there is a ninety-eight percent probability you are the deceased child's mother."

Margo burst into tears. She pulled a tissue from her purse and held it to her face.

Her lawyer stood. "That's enough for today. Mrs. Lumpas is upset that you may be accusing her of several possible criminal scenarios, when the science on which you're basing those accusations admits it is less than one hundred percent accurate. We're out of here, officers."

Freeborn helped Margo out of her chair and escorted her out of the interrogation room.

I could hear her sniffling all the way out the building. "Well, what does her behavior tell you?" I asked.

"Maybe guilty of something, but maybe protecting the guilty party. Who knows?" Tuttle replied. "You didn't get much, did you?"

"Not as much as I had hoped for, but enough to let me know I'm on the right track."

Chapter 11

Special Agent Mona Casola carefully studied the report which had come to her from the FBI Crime Lab. When she was certain, she punched my number into her cell phone. The phone rang three times and then went to voicemail. She waited until the recorded message ended and she heard the phone beep.

"This is Special Agent Casola, FBI. We spoke a couple of weeks ago about the possible mother of your baby John Doe. Hope that's going well. Gimme a call when you've got a minute. I think we may have ID'd the father. You'll have to work with me on this one because he's out of state from you. Looks like 'FBI to the rescue.' You've got my number."

At nine at night, her cell phone rang. "Damn, I forgot to turn my phone off," she said. She shut off the shower, wrapped herself in an old beach towel, and lifted her phone from the vanity in her bathroom. "Casola here."

"Sorry to call so late. This is Bart Jones from Willow Falls."

Agent Casola sounded befuddled. "Jeezuz. Gimme a few minutes and I'll call you back."

"Want me to call you tomorrow morning?"

"No. I've got time now. I just need a few minutes to dry off. You caught me in the shower."

"Okay, sorry." I canceled the call. I felt foolish for

having called so late, but I was excited I might have another avenue to solving the BabyX case. I went into my kitchen and pulled a bottle of beer out of my refrigerator. The first swallow was very cold and caused my throat to spasm shut. Of course, that was the moment Agent Casola returned my call.

"Hallaugh?"

"Is that you, Bart? Do I have the right number?"

"Yaaah."

"Want me to call back?"

There was a long pause and then my voice came through, sounding a little more normal. "Sorry. You know how a cold liquid can cause your throat to close?"

"Beer?"

"Yeah."

"I'd tell you that you shouldn't drink late at night, but I'm guilty of it myself."

"What do you have for me?"

The tone of Agent Casola's voice changed to one of pride, maybe delight. "FBI scores again…we got a name for the probable father of your BabyX."

"That's what your voice mail told me. Can you give me the name?"

"Michael Anthony Agosta. Does it mean anything to you?"

"Nope, not yet. Do you mind hanging on while I check a high school yearbook?"

"I'll be right here when you get back."

I found the 2000 Willow Falls Golden Eagles yearbook in my briefcase, then checked all four grades. Nothing.

"I thought I might have had him and his picture in the high school yearbook, but he isn't there. Maybe he attended school in a different district."

"Maybe he already graduated. Maybe he was in middle school. Maybe he was her teacher or a neighbor. Maybe he was military on leave and hitting on a local gal…You have a bunch of possible scenarios, Bart."

"Would you send me what you have on him? I'd like to interview the probable mother again."

"Will do. Meanwhile, since he's possibly implicated in a wrongful death, I'm flying to down to interrogate him in three days. Get this: He's a Judge in Kanawha County, West Virginia. A judge!"

I could not believe my ears. "Really? A judge?"

"It gets better. He's running on both the Conservative and Republican tickets for a vacant seat on the West Virginia State Supreme Court of Appeals. Right now he's eight points ahead of his Democratic rival. Election's the fourth of November."

"If I can squeeze airfare out of my chief, can I join you for the interrogation?"

"Yeah. I'd like to meet you. My boyfriend just dumped me, so hanging around with a married man might up my image with the scumbags around here."

"Send me your flight details, and I'll try to get there around the same time."

****

I stopped by to see Assistant Superintendent Elise Grogan again. Her office seemed extraordinarily busy, with both Mrs. Grogan and her secretary on separate phones barking orders at people on the other end.

When the secretary hung up, she gave me a "what do *you* want?" look before she composed herself and told me quietly they were busy dealing with the fallout of a shooting in a neighborhood near one of the district's elementary schools. "Things seem to have calmed down now. You wouldn't have wanted to be us half an hour ago."

Mrs. Grogan looked up and saw me standing at her secretary's desk. I raised my hand in a meek wave. She hung up and straightened her sweater before walking out of the office to greet me. She was wearing the same outfit as the first time we had met.

"I can give you a couple of minutes. That's all," she said

"Sorry to arrive unannounced at an inconvenient time. I thought I'd return your 2000 yearbook."

"Why, thank you. I didn't expect it back so soon. I thought it might become State's evidence."

"Not yet. Would you mind if I checked a couple of others? I'm looking for a young man named Michael Anthony Agosta. He could have graduated a few years earlier or maybe even a few later."

I followed Grogan as she marched into her office, where she pulled half a dozen yearbooks from her bookshelf and blew the dust off them. "These haven't seen such use in a very long time."

We each took a yearbook and began looking for Michael Agosta. It didn't take long before Mrs. Grogran said, "Found him. He was a junior in 1999. He doesn't appear as a senior in 2000." She handed me the yearbook so I could see Agosta's high school photo.

"Maybe his parents moved to West Virginia."

"Why West Virginia?"

"That's where he's living now."

I asked Ms. Grogan if she would photocopy Michael's picture. She agreed and gave me three copies.

Chapter 12

Two days later, I flew from Albany to Charleston, West Virginia. As I walked out of the "Arrivals" tunnel, I was met by a man and a woman dressed in black suits. The woman was holding a paper plate on which she had scrawled the word BART in blue ballpoint pen. Even in her suit, I could tell she was muscular and probably worked out regularly. Her chestnut brown hair was cut chin length and hung straight. Her makeup was basic.

"Agent Casola?" I asked.

"So, you're Bart. You look different from how I had imagined. Thought you might have been younger. No offense."

"And I thought you'd be older. You aren't a day over thirty-five."

"Watch it, buck-o. I'm twenty-nine."

"Then I was right."

Agent Casola introduced me to Special Agent Paul Maxwell of the Charleston, West Virginia, FBI office. He would be our driver and ombudsman as we coordinated our investigation with the Charleston Police Department. Maxwell had called ahead and arranged a special meeting with His Honor Michael Agosta.

Michael was waiting in the interview room at the Charleston PD when we arrived. He was dressed in a gray tweed sportscoat and black slacks. His red and silver striped tie was loosened at the collar.

Introductions were made and then questions began.

"Do you know why we've asked to speak with you, your honor?" I began.

Michael looked me in the eyes, studying me. He'd dealt with many policemen before, but always from the position of prosecutor or judge. Sitting as a defendant was both demeaning and improper for a man of his position. "None whatsoever."

"And you've waived your right to counsel…"

"Yes." Agosta shrugged. "I have nothing to hide. What is it I'm accused of?"

"Think of this as exploratory," Agent Casola said. "Detective Jones has some interesting information to share with you."

"Did the Democrats put you up to this?"

"Not unless they have an 'in' with the FBI's DNA analysis lab," Casola replied.

I related the same information I had shared with Margo Lumpas, but without mentioning her. "…and the FBI analysis indicates ninety-eight percent probability you are BabyX's father."

Michael slumped in his chair, clearly puzzled. "This is impossible. My wife and I didn't have children until I was in college. There must be a mistake."

"You're a judge, your honor. DNA analyses are commonly accepted as evidence in most courts of law, especially in paternity cases. This one nails you as the father."

"But I left Willow Falls at the end of my junior year in high school. I wasn't even dating anybody back then." A rush of horror ran through his veins as he remembered Margo.

I saw Michael's irises open wide and decided to drive right at the subject rather than play around until something trapped the judge into an admission of paternity. "Does the name Margo Lumpas mean anything to you?"

Judge Agosta shook his head. "Not at all."

"Does the name Margo Borst mean anything to you?"

The judge slumped farther in his chair. "Yes. She was a girl I was friends with during my junior year."

I scrawled the words "F_ck Friends" on a sheet of paper and slid it across the table to Agosta. "Does this term mean anything to you?"

The judge straightened up. "Did she tell you that?"

"Nope. But I saw it scrawled in a high school yearbook and had to look up the term online."

"Were you bopping that girl during your junior year?" Agent Casola asked.

The judge put his head into his hands. When he raised his head, Casola and I could see the look of horror on his face. "Are you telling me Margo was pregnant when my family left Willow Falls?"

"No, but it's clearly one possible assumption," Agent Casola replied.

I put my digital recorder on the table. "Do you mind if I tape this?"

The judge shook his head in disbelief. "Oh God." He could see his career cascading down like an avalanche, his family embarrassed, his election in shambles.

"Tell us about it," Agent Casola said.

"So, I guess you know what an 'FF' is. It's the abbreviation we kids used back then. It started becoming popular when I was in my teens. I guess it's sort of rampant now—they call it 'friends with benefits'—but back then it was new and intriguing. It was a way to become good at the sex act, so when you'd meet the person of your dreams, you'd know what to do and how not to be clumsy at sex."

"Did it live up to its promise?" I asked. There was something sexually intriguing in the possibility.

"For me, I guess so. I met my wife at a party when I was a freshman at Marshall University. She had just graduated and had landed a first-grade teaching position in an elementary school in town. It was her first year as a teacher. Things clicked between us and we were sleeping together pretty soon thereafter. There's no doubt that without an FF in high school, I'd never have appealed to Audrey, my wife. We got married when I was a senior. She was six months pregnant, but she managed to finish out the year before our daughter was born."

"Were you there for the delivery?" Agent Casola asked.

The judge cocked his head in disbelief of the assertion. "Yes, of course. It's the decent thing to do."

"Were you there when BabyX was born?" I asked.

The judge shook his head. "I didn't know there *was* a BabyX until right now. I'm shocked and mortified. How's my wife going to take this? To what end will the press go to embarrass my family and humiliate me? For God's sake, I'm running for the State Supreme Court of Appeals. The election is in just a few weeks."

"We know," Agent Casola said. "That's why we asked to meet you here. You should probably hire an attorney and prepare your wife for the worst. We don't know where this is going at the moment, but there's the distinct possibility of a murder charge against you, your high school FF, or both of you."

"I assure you on my word of honor as a representative of the West Virginia legal justice system that the DNA analysis may have found me guilty of fathering that poor child, but I had no knowledge of his existence until today, and most certainly I didn't murder him."

After the judge left, Special Agent Maxwell asked, "Do you believe him?"

"It's hard not to," I said.

"He's probably a liar," Agent Casola sneered. "All men are."

Chapter 13

Margo Lumpas arrived home at one in the afternoon. Her meeting at the Marshfield Police Department had gone worse than she had imagined. The police knew more about her past than she had thought possible and all because she had agreed to help her husband with the development of a new DNA learning module at Marshfield High School. It was so unjust, so unfair for someone to drag her ugly past into the joy of her present life. It was the worst form of mudslinging, and she was not even anybody important. She did not want to be thrust centerstage in a tidal wave of poor decisions from her past.

She and Lance Freeborn had left the meeting after only a few questions, Freeborn calling it to a quick end because of the self-incrimination aspect of the questions I had been hurling at her. After the meeting, Freeborn had taken her to a local diner in Willow Falls near the Marshfield border, where he bought her a cup of coffee and talked her down from her case of nervous anxiety.

Following Lance Freeborn's suggestion, Margo resigned herself to her fate: She had to come clean with her husband, to tell him the truth about her youthful mistake and its painful outcome. How was she going to be able to do that? Margo wished her husband had never asked her to participate in the DNA analysis of their family's heritage because modern science now had found a way to pry open the past and expose it to the world. Suddenly, she was no longer able to hide her past behind the security and façade of her life as a loving wife and mother in a middle-class neighborhood.

When she first had met him, Henry Lumpas was both a widower and a struggling single father. He was drowning in work at the high school, where he taught three courses and two science labs per day, five days per week. He needed assistance with caring for a toddler, as well as light housework and cooking, but on his educator's salary, he could not afford professional help. His mortgage, car payment, and college loan ate most of his paycheck.

The job he offered Margo paid less than minimum wage, but it included room and board. He gave her a room directly across the hall from little Raina, named after his wife's mother, now deceased from a losing battle with breast cancer. As part of the arrangement, when Henry got home from work each afternoon, Margo would attend evening classes at the regional community college. During the day, she would study and/or clean house and do laundry when Raina took her nap.

It was a mutually beneficial employment arrangement. Margo's coursework went well and her skills as a daycare provider did not go unnoticed. Raina played with Margo all day every day and grew to love her as she would have loved her own mother. And over time, Margo's employee-employer relationship with Henry turned to friendship. He advised her through her coursework at the college and applauded loudly when Margo walked across the stage in cap and gown at her commencement ceremony. And friendship eventually turned to love, unspoken at first, then spoken, and then it became a passionate relationship, and ultimately, Margo never needed to change the sheets in her bedroom across the hall.

When Margo discovered she was with child, Henry did not hesitate to whisk her down to the Willow Falls City Clerk's Office and arrange for a civil ceremony, conducted two days later. They honeymooned for a weekend in Lake Placid, and then returned to their daily lives, where Margo's weekly paychecks ended because she was no longer an employee. She missed the money, but she managed to squeeze a little personal cash from the allowance Henry gave her for groceries and cleaning supplies.

Zoe was born when Raina was five. Little Louie was born almost three years later. To anyone looking at them from an outside perspective, Margo and Henry were devoted parents to their three kids, and their family unit was strong. And only a few neighbors knew Henry was ten years older than Margo and that she had won his heart by caring for the daughter from his first marriage.

****

Henry arrived home from work at four in the afternoon. Margo had prepared his favorite dish for dinner, lemon chicken with wild rice. She also had put a two-liter bottle of chardonnay in the freezer to chill.

"Where are the kids?" he asked, plopping his briefcase on a kitchen chair.

"Your sister has them tonight. She'll be bringing them home around nine."

Henry's sister was a registered nurse, who lived a few miles away in the Town of Glen Arbor, and who worked part-time at the county nursing home. After a long and bitter divorce battle, she had managed to escape with the family's small Craftsman home and a monthly support check which more than covered all her expenses. Childless, she loved to watch the Lumpas' children, and tonight was an important night, so Margo pawned Zoe and little Louie off on her.

Margo offered Henry a glass of Chardonnay, which he gladly accepted. During dinner she drank three glasses to his two, but he did not criticize because some days are just harder at home for a wife and mother than they are for a husband away at work. Besides, with the kids gone for the evening and with a special meal prepared, Henry suspected his wife planned to become amorous.

After she cleaned the table and put the dishes in the sink, Margo took Henry by the hand and led him into the living room. "We need to talk," she said. Her voice was weak. She sat on their reupholstered sofa and motioned for him to sit beside her. "This is going to be hard for me, Henry. I need you to listen carefully and not be critical of me."

Henry broke into a smile. "You're not leaving me, are you?"

Margo's hands shook. Her neck was spotted with red. Her voice quavered. "You may want me to leave after what I have to say."

Henry swallowed, knowing something horrific was headed his way. "Go on and tell me, now that you have my stomach in a knot."

Margo's eyes filled with tears. She wrung her hands. "I was involved in something terrible before you knew me, Henry." She stood and walked to the oaken mantel of their red-brick fireplace. "It's something I've never told you or anyone else about because it was something I wasn't proud of. In fact, I feel ashamed about it every day of my life."

Henry lay back against the soft brown cushion of the sofa, his shoulders slumped and his mind racing over all the possible scenarios his wife might describe. He started to say something, but Margo raised her palm and shushed him. Then she pulled a tissue from a box on the glass-top coffee table and blew her nose.

"Were you in a Willow Falls gang?" he asked.

"I wish," she replied, her hands still shaking. "It's nothing so glamorous."

Margo blew her nose again, and then patted tears from her eyes. As she removed the tissue, more tears streamed down her cheeks. "My DNA report came the other day. It exposed something horrific from my past."

Henry was beside himself with anxiety and wished his wife would get on with whatever was going to ruin his evening. The Yankees game was scheduled to be televised at eight. "Was your grandfather a murderer?"

Margo wiped her eyes and blew her nose again. She threw the used tissue onto the coffee table and pulled another from the box. "Henry, please. This is hard enough without your constant interruptions."

Henry quieted.

"You know I wasn't a virgin when I married you. Neither were you when you married your first wife." She wrung her hands and spoke with measured words. "Back when I was a junior in high school, I gave birth to a child, a little boy."

For a moment, Henry was shocked, but he gained his composure quickly, realizing that the "BabyX" in little Louie's DNA report was probably his wife's child from a teenage fling. He rose and held out his arms. "Has he reached out to you?"

Margo's eyes erupted and she wailed. Henry took her into his arms. "It's okay, sweetheart. You know everything we did before we knew each other is forgiven. It's always been that way."

Margo took several deep breaths. "It's nice of you to remind me of that agreement, but there's more."

Henry sat back against the sofa again, his eyes wide with concern.

"I didn't know I was pregnant. I had my period every month. Then one day I went into labor and delivered the child. He was stillborn." She blew her nose, tears streaming onto the top of the tissue.

"That must have been terrible for you, especially losing the child in such a way."

Margo pulled another tissue from the box. She wailed again, then took several deep breaths. "I was stupid, Henry, a teenager with nowhere to turn."

"How did your parents react? They're so conservative."

"They weren't there when the baby was born. I delivered it alone, upstairs in an abandoned house."

"Oh God," Henry moaned. "You're torturing me."

Margo sobbed and began hiccupping. Henry hurried to the kitchen and returned with a tall glass of cold water. He handed it to Margo and kissed her neck. "This must have haunted you for all these years.

"There's more, Henry."

Henry sat back down and rubbed his forehead, unsure what could be more horrible.

"When the baby arrived, I was shocked. I didn't

know what to do. It was hours before I recognized the baby wasn't crying…that he was dead. I couldn't tell my parents because they'd throw me out like they did my sister. With nowhere to turn, I buried the baby in a shallow grave…"

Henry gasped.

"…in the dirt-floor basement of the abandoned house."

Henry felt his world crashing down. "Oh God."

Margo's tears began to dry. She had gotten it out. Now there was no secret hiding between her and her husband. He knew the worst of it. How would he react when the truth of it all came to rest inside his head?

Henry's face was in his hands.

"Now listen carefully to me, Henry."

"Oh God," he said again.

"So, they were doing a neighborhood renewal project in Willow Falls last year and discovered the skeleton. They ran a DNA analysis and it matched with my DNA, the DNA sample you asked me to give for your project."

Henry broke into a sweat. His eyes flicked from side to side.

"Today I was called into the Marshfield Police Department where I was questioned by a detective from Willow Falls."

Henry removed his face from his hands and looked at his wife. His eyes were tearing. "We need to get you an attorney…"

Margo nodded. "I know. I've already contracted with Lance Freeborn. I heard he's the best."

Henry was puzzled. He felt as though the woman standing before him was not the same Margo he had married. "You did all of this, the contracting with the attorney and the questioning at the police station, without telling me?"

Margo burst into tears again. Holding a tissue against her eyes with both hands, she nodded her head quickly. "Yes. I'm a miserable person and a horrible wife. I've been living with this horrible nightmare all my life. I should have told you about it before we were married. I certainly wish I had. If you want me to leave, I'll understand."

Henry felt betrayed, but he still adored Margo. She was the mother of two of his children. He needed her. Their kids needed her. "Nice try, but you aren't getting off that easily. Have they charged you with anything?"

"The detective said the evidence might lead to a charge of murder, but I reassured him that the baby was stillborn."

"And what about the father? Have you contacted him? What did he say when you gave birth back in high school?"

Margo blew her nose again. "He wasn't there. He doesn't even know."

"How…?"

"He was seventeen. His father was transferred to Ohio, and he left Willow Falls before I even knew I was pregnant. I have no idea where he is now, or what he's doing."

"We have to think this thing through," Henry said. "This is a small community. We have position and reputation to consider." He drummed his fingers on the arm of the sofa. "How long did you date him?"

"We never really dated."

"So, you just slept with him?" Henry asked in an

accusatory tone.

Margo had nothing left to say. If she told Henry that she and Michael had been FFs, he'd think she was a whore. It might even end their marriage. So, she lied. "It wasn't like that. I didn't just sleep with him."

Henry was confused. "I don't understand."

Margo's mind spun uncontrollably. How could she save face? How could she save her marriage? Then it just slipped out. "He raped me."

Henry's expression changed from suspicion to compassion "Raped you? Oh God, sweetheart. No wonder you couldn't tell me. How horrible to live all your adult life with that hanging over you." Henry hugged his wife again and kissed her salty cheeks and lips. "How horrible to be raped and then to deliver a stillborn child and never to tell anyone about it." Henry thought quietly for a moment and then cocked his head. "He raped you and you didn't tell the police or even a high school guidance counselor?"

Margo pulled another tissue from the box and dried her eyes. "He was from a richer family. Who would they believe…me or him?" She paused to catch her breath and then the story spun out of control. "Besides, it wasn't a single incident. He raped me multiple times."

"Oh my God," Henry gasped. "You poor thing. I'm sorry you never told me so you could get it out."

Margo shook uncontrollably. "It was horrible. He threatened to ruin my reputation, to tell my parents and all the other kids in school that I was a whore." Margo wailed again. "It was horrible, I tell you."

"I'm sorry you've had to live with this, Margo. But we'll get by this together, like we've gotten by other issues we've faced." Henry pounded his fist into a decorator pillow which lay against the arm of the sofa. "I hope that bastard gets what's coming to him."

Chapter 14

Special Agent Mona Casola was sitting at a bar in the Yeager Airport, six miles from Charleston, WV, waiting for her flight back to D.C. She was on her third beer. I was sitting beside her, dressed in the same charcoal gray suit I had been wearing all day and nursing my second rye and ginger. I was flying back to the airport at Albany, NY.

"You seem to have an ugly opinion of men, Agent Casola."

"Call me 'Mona.' I think we've known each other long enough, and you don't seem to be the type who wants to get into my pants."

I tilted my drink at a forty-five-degree angle. "You don't mince words, do you, Mona?"

"For a young woman, I've been mistreated by enough bozos to turn any female into a man-hater."

"I gathered that back in Charleston, when you said all men are liars."

Agent Casola finished her third beer and signaled to the bartender that she would do one more. "I guess I was a little harsh. I should have said *most* men are liars. It's not all of you...just most."

"That's hurtful to my peers and my masculine self-concept."

"Look, it's a matter of personal history. First, there was this guy back in college named Benny Dix. We dated for almost three months before I let him score. He told me I was his first, but it took another three months of penicillin to kill the stuff he gave me.

"Then there was a guy I really liked. Randy traveled a lot because he was a pharmaceuticals rep. I might have fallen deeper in love with him, but I discovered he already had two wives, one in California and one in Baltimore. He's doing time for bigamy."

"He probably deserved it," I said. "Did you deliver the arrest warrant?"

"You bet your sweet ass. I collared him myself and drove him to the police for processing."

The bartender delivered Agent Casola's fourth beer and took a twenty off the bar to ring up the sale.

"Then I fell bigtime for a guy named Dan Arrow." She took a swig of beer. "You ever meet someone, and you know it's right?"

"Well, I felt that way about my wife, Rachel. A few dates with her and I knew we were perfect for each other. I think she felt it, too."

"Danny didn't know shit when it hit him in the face."

I shrugged my shoulders. "Sorry…"

"Danny is a private detective with an office in D.C. He called the FBI in on a case he was working. It was a missing persons incident that morphed into kidnapping with interstate implications. Headquarters tapped me as his federal assistance. The case took us to several states before we solved it. I was in love with him from the third or fourth day we were together. I thought he felt the same way. We shouldn't have, but we started sleeping together. It broke all the regulations, if you know what I mean."

I simply nodded. I was going to hear a tale of unrequited love.

Agent Casola chugged her fourth beer to the half-empty mark. She belched loud and long enough to draw stares from the men seated nearby. "So there we were, investigating all day and screwing all night. The day we solved the case, he was wrestling with the kidnapper and lost his pistol. I pulled my piece and ordered the kidnapper to stop, but he got Danny in a full-nelson and ordered me to drop my weapon, or he'd kill Danny. I did as I was asked. The kidnapper let Danny go and walked over to pick up my piece. When he looked away for half a moment, Danny pulled a small Beretta from his ankle holster and plugged the guy in the head."

"Good shot with such a small pistol."

"Yeah, it was. So, that night when we made love, I told Danny I loved him. I thought it was time." She paused for a moment and frowned. "He told me I shouldn't have said that."

"Sounds like he was using you."

"I don't think so. I just think he was afraid of love. Probably still is."

I finished my drink. "So, what happened then?"

"Nothing. After I told him I loved him, he disappeared. He never called me again. He never answered my calls. Son of a bitch. I hate him."

"You still love him, don't you?"

Agent Casola chugged the remainder of her beer. "Probably…"

Chapter 15

When I returned to Willow Falls, I called Chief Parillo and asked for a second meeting with Margo Lumpas.

"You got more to ask her?" the chief asked.

"Yeah, I went to West Virginia and met the father of the baby. I need to verify some facts."

"Anything you can tell me now?"

I wondered if Chief Parillo might be passing information along to Mrs. Lumpas or her attorney. "The FBI has asked me to keep this info close to my chest," I lied. "I've got to honor their request."

"All right, I'll see if I can set something up."

Two hours later, Chief Parillo called. "Mrs. Lumpas will meet with you at the Marshfield PD headquarters at four o'clock on Thursday afternoon."

"Thanks, Chief." It seemed late for a meeting, especially for a woman with school-aged children, but I was happy to have the interview.

On Thursday, I arrived half an hour early and was escorted into the interrogation room by the same officer who had been reading the magazine article comparing the behaviors of chimpanzees and humans. A few minutes later Patrolman Tuttle arrived, looking the same as she had for the first interview, except her shoulder length hair was down. I noted streaks of gray in it. "You didn't bring your female representative," she said. "What was her name…Martin?"

"Nope, I didn't bring Helen Martin. She's got an elderly mother and this meeting is too late for her evening duties. I thought you'd do. You're as much my witness as you are Mrs. Lumpas'"

"That's good by me. I get paid by the hour, so the longer you interview her, the better for me."

The door opened. Two men walked in, followed by Margo Lumpas. The first man was her attorney, Lance Freeborn, dressed in the same blue pin-striped suit as the time before, but this time he was wearing a hot pink tie. The other guy looked nervous and out of place. He was wearing tan slacks and a short sleeve white golf shirt which clung awkwardly to his undershirt.

Lace Freeborn spoke first. "My client asked to bring her husband along for today's questioning."

I extended my hand, but Henry Lumpas refused to shake it.

"Mr. Lumpas is aware of the details you divulged at our last meeting. He fully supports his wife's explanation of the baby's birth and death."

"I would expect that of a loving husband," I replied.

"So, what new information do you have to share?" Freeborn asked, opening a leather notebook.

"I only have a few new questions to ask." I removed the small digital recorder from my pocket and set it on the table. "Since our last meeting, I've had the opportunity to interview BabyX's father."

Margo burst into tears. Her husband handed her a tissue from a small packet he held in his hands.

"He's a county judge in West Virginia. He's a nice man…respectable, like you."

Margo blew her nose.

"He remembers you, Mrs. Lumpas, and admits to the possibility of being BabyX's father, although he had no knowledge of your pregnancy until I spoke with him a few days ago."

Margo sniveled. "I know the baby was mine. You don't have to tell me that. The DNA analysis was correct."

"He says when he was seventeen and you were sixteen, the two of you entered into an 'FF' relationship from which both of you hoped to gain sexual experience and skill in the sex act." I jotted the two-word meaning of "FF" on a piece of paper and slid it toward Margo Lumpas. "You remember what 'FF' means, don't you?"

Margo nodded her head and wailed. Mr. Lumpas took her hand. "It's okay, sweetheart. I'm here to help you through this. Tell them what you told me."

It took a full minute for Margo to regain her composure so she could speak.

"We didn't have that kind of relationship...the kind you described," she finally said.

"So, what kind of relationship *did* you have?"

She blew her nose into the tissue and reached for another. "We lived in the same neighborhood, and we were in school together. One day in the summer he took me to see an abandoned house over near the cemetery. He broke in through the back and then opened the kitchen door so I could go in. I shouldn't have, but I did. The house was empty, except for a bedroom upstairs where there was a mattress and a chair..." Tears streamed down her cheeks and onto the collar of her blue blouse.

"Go on, sweetheart," Henry Lumpas said. "It's okay."

"He pushed me down on the mattress and raped me." Her tears and sobs grew heavier.

I was perplexed by her long answer. It seemed too contrived. "But when did you have the baby?"

"When I was a junior."

"But when?"

"The baby was born in the Fall of 2000. I don't remember the date."

"So, you're saying your pregnancy was about fifteen months long."

Margo pulled another tissue from the packet in her husband's hand and blew her nose. "No, I don't know when I got pregnant…probably sometime in the late spring or early summer of 2000."

"I don't understand," I said, trying to decipher what she had told me.

"Listen, that bastard raped my wife repeatedly all year long," Henry Lumpas blurted.

Lance Feeborn took Mr. Lumpas by the arm. "This has to be her testimony. Your outbursts aren't helping her cause."

Mr. Lumpas snorted and then pressed his back into his chair.

"Is that right? Are you telling me Michael Agosta raped you repeatedly during your sophomore year in high school?"

She nodded her head while holding a tissue to her nose.

"Tell me about it. How can that be?"

"After he raped me the first time, he told me if I told anyone, he'd tell all the kids in school I paid him to have sex with me and that I was a whore. He even kept my underwear as a trophy to show everyone that he was telling them the truth."

"How many times did he force himself upon you?" Patrolman Tuttle asked.

Margo burst into sobs. "Almost…almost every week…for the entire school year."

"Jesus," Tuttle said, throwing her pencil onto the table.

"How can that be?" I asked. Margo Lumpas wasn't making any sense.

"I was afraid to tell my parents because of what he would say about me. They were very conservative, and they would have disowned me, like they did my sister when she got pregnant."

Henry Lumpas leaned over and kissed his wife's cheek. "Go on. It'll help you to get it all out, sweetheart."

Margo nodded and wiped her nose. She told me the same lie she had told her husband. She was in too deep to change her story. "Michael would just take me to that same abandoned house and force me to undress and then he'd have his way with me. It was awful."

"When did the continuing rapes end?" I asked.

"When his father was transferred to Ohio. Before the baby was born."

"You must have felt relief when he finally was gone," Tuttle said.

Margo nodded. "Yes. It ended the nightmare."

The questions ended and the room grew quiet. After half a minute, Margo sobbed again.

Patrolman Tuttle left the room for a moment and returned with a freshly opened box of tissues. Margo took two.

I went back to business with my questions. "So, when was the baby born?"

Margo put her trembling hand on the table. "In the fall. I don't remember what month."

"Was it before or after Halloween?"

"I don't remember. It was cool, but not cold weather. It hadn't snowed yet."

"What else do you recall?"

"I had gone to the store for something, and my contractions started when I was coming home." She reached for another tissue, her hand still trembling uncontrollably.

"Go on," I told her.

"I went to the house where Michael would take me to rape me and laid down on that same mattress."

I was stymied by her response. "Why there?"

"I was afraid to go home because my parents weren't there, and my sister was entertaining her boyfriend." She paused for a moment and took two deep breaths. "I didn't know I was pregnant. I thought I had food poisoning. But the baby came. It was so very tiny, and it was born dead."

"How would you know that?"

When the baby was born, Margo had lifted it to her chest to embrace it and had wiped the mayonnaise off its face with her skirt. At the time she had not known that babies are born bluish gray. She also had not known what to do with the umbilical cord.

"It didn't breathe, and it never cried," she said, her eyes looking away, somewhere in the past.

"You've had other children since then?" Tuttle asked.

"Yes, two. A girl and a boy."

"How did that baby compare to the ones you had in the hospital?"

Margo sat quietly for a moment. "My children since then both cried immediately upon delivery. Henry was there. He'll tell you it's true."

Henry nodded. "Louie was really loud when he cried."

Margo's attorney touched his arm and Henry sat back against his chair again.

"They were at least two or three times as large as the baby boy. He couldn't have weighed more than a pound or two."

"What did you do with him?" Tuttle asked.

Margo had wrapped the dead baby and its placenta in a plastic bag she had gotten at the drugstore. She said a prayer over the grave, placed the body in a hole she had dug with a garden trowel, and packed dirt over it.

She sobbed again. "I had just turned seventeen. I didn't know what to do with the body, so I just buried it."

"Where?" I asked.

"In the basement of the house. It had a dirt floor."

"Then what did you do?"

Margo inhaled and blew out the air. "Then I went home and took a shower."

"What did you tell your parents?"

"My parents didn't get home until late. They never knew. I never told them. I was ashamed to have been some boy's 'punch'…I think that's what they called it on those police shows on television back then."

"So, do you want to formally accuse Michael Agosta of rape?" I asked.

"Of course, she does," Henry Lumpas exclaimed.

Margo's attorney grabbed his arm again. "This is the last time I want to speak with you about putting words in Mrs. Lumpas' mouth. You're not helping her and you're certainly not helping your family with these outbursts."

Margo sat quietly for a moment. "Oh, I don't know. It was so long ago," Margo said. "I don't want the newspapers to paste my picture all over the place. What would my children think? Our neighbors? Besides, isn't there a time limit on that sort of thing?"

"They call it 'statute of limitations,'" I said, "and no, there's no time limit on rape. Ask Bill Clinton or Harvey Weinstein."

"I don't know…"

"Of course, she does," Henry Lumpas repeated.

Chapter 16

Almost three weeks passed before Judge Michael Agosta was arrested for rape. First, the Willow Falls District Attorney had to pull together a Grand Jury to hear Margo's testimony about her multiple rapes and the ultimate delivery of the stillborn child. Then the Grand Jury heard testimony from Armando Lambrucci, who dug up the skeleton, and discussed a deposition from the FBI's DNA lab that cross-checked the skeleton's DNA against the results of all major commercial DNA analysis outfits. All fingers pointed at Michael, so the Grand Jury decided he must be arrested and stand trial for his sins.

Paperwork had to be drafted and cooperative arrangements needed to be made between the FBI and the Charleston, West Virginia PD so each party knew its responsibilities and charges. Someone in the Charleston police department tipped off the Democrat Party. In turn, they tipped off the press, and before the police and FBI arrived to arrest His Honor, at least a dozen reporters and three television trucks were parked outside the courthouse where Judge Agosta worked.

Judge Agosta was entering the courtroom from his chambers when the arrest took place. Seated at their respective tables in the front, the defendants and prosecutors for the case got a good look at justice in overdrive.

"Judge Michael Agosta?" an FBI agent asked.

"Yes, can I help you? If this is about an upcoming case, please see the clerk."

Two special agents stepped in front of the defendant's table. Both were wearing navy blue suits, and both showed their badges. The shorter and thinner of the two was the spokesperson. He pulled his ID out of his coat pocket and showed it again to the judge. "I'm from the Federal Bureau of Investigation, here to arrest you on the charges of repeated aggravated assault and rape. You can come with me peacefully, or you can wear cuffs."

Michael's jaw dropped.

"You have the right to remain silent. Anything you say can and will be used against you in a court of law. You have the right to an attorney. If you cannot afford an attorney, one will be provided for you. Do you understand these Rights?"

"This is preposterous," Michael exclaimed. "You can't do this here or now. I'm scheduled to hear this case. See me in my Chambers later this afternoon. You're grandstanding."

The bulkier of the two FBI agents spun Michael around, pulled his hands behind him, and fitted nylon cuffs on his wrists. Then he quickly patted Michael down.

"What about our case?" one of the prosecutors asked. "We've been readying for six months, and we're scheduled for a hearing today."

"Take it up with the Clerk of the Court," the smaller FBI agent said. "His Honor here has been arrested and won't be sitting on the bench for a while."

The two agents led Judge Agosta briskly through

the gray marble hallways of the courthouse and then down the wide granite stairway which led to the street where a black Chevy Suburban was waiting, it's motor running. As they neared the Suburban, the dozen reporters swarmed over to ask questions. "Why have you been arrested, Your Honor?" "How many women have you raped, Your Honor?" "What effect will your arrest have upon your election, Your Honor?"

"I'm innocent of any and all charges," Michael announced. "This is a ploy by my opponents to interfere with the election process and my candidacy. If you can't beat them honestly, destroy their character and humiliate them in public. This is a lynch mob. This is Democrat Party behavior at its worst."

The larger of the two FBI agents pushed down on Michael's head and dumped him into the back seat of the Suburban. He slammed the door shut, and then then he walked briskly around the vehicle and climbed in beside Michael.

The smaller FBI agent turned to the reporters. "His Honor has been arrested. The Chief of Police and other FBI officials will be making a statement at noon today. I suggest that you disband from here and reassemble at the police department if you want a good seat." Then he climbed into the front passenger seat and the Suburban left the area.

****

Mona Casola leaned against a polished marble wall and punched my number into her cell phone.

I had just arrived at work after a brief meeting with a housewife who did not remember Margo Borst. The plastic cap was still on the cup of coffee I had purchased at the newsstand outside the police station. I set it on my desk when my cell phone started ringing,

"Is that you, Jones? Mona Casola here."

"How's it going?" I asked.

"I'm in Charleston. It's done. He was brought in and is now in processing. He isn't happy."

I pulled the tab back on my coffee lid and took a sip. The coffee was black and hot, the way I like it. "Did he come peacefully?"

"He was in cuffs."

"Not too good for his public image."

"Probably not. I'd guess his campaign for the Court of Appeals just rolled off the bridge."

"Too bad. He seemed like an upright person when we interviewed him. But then, so did she."

"They both tell a convincing tale. It's going to be up to the court system to decide who's telling the truth." Mona paused for a moment. It sounded like she was chugging a beer again, but it was only ten in the morning. "They still got you continuing to dig up evidence?" she asked when the glugging sound stopped.

"Yeah. Looks like I'll be on it for quite a while. My current mission is finding everybody who knew either of them and discovering anything which might shed light on the truth."

"What about the bones?" Casola asked.

"Social Services is working with a couple of churches to raise money to give the little guy a decent funeral. You think the parents might chip in?"

"I'm guessing not. I think they're going to be up to their eyeballs in litigation costs."

"What's next for you?" I asked.

"More paperwork and negotiations. We've got to help the Charleston PD extradite him back to Willow

Falls for trial. That'll take a few days. I may get stuck with the road trip to bring him to you. Hopefully, we can fly. Meanwhile, there's a rumor his attorney is going to sue the Willow Falls PD and the FBI for wrongful arrest. If that happens, it might delay his extradition by a few months."

****

Audrey Agosta was tying the bow on the thirty-seventh bag of homemade cowboy cookies when her phone rang. The cookies were intended as token gifts for Friday night's "thank you" supper for the volunteers who had been working on Michael's campaign. She plopped the clear plastic bag with its hand-tied red bow into the cardboard box which sat on a kitchen stool, and then she answered the phone. "Campaign headquarters."

"This is William Teal of the Charleston Gazette. I was wondering if I might quote you in my article on your husband's arrest?"

"Excuse me?" she asked.

"Your husband's arrest this morning. Do you have anything to say about it?"

"Is this April Fool's Day?"

"You don't know about it, do you?" Teal determined quickly. "He was arrested today for rape. Would you like to comment on his arrest?"

Audrey hung up the phone. It rang almost immediately. "Hello?" she asked.

"Mrs. Agosta, my name is Clara Hawthorne with the Bluefield Daily Telegraph. I'm wondering if you can illuminate me on the charges brought against your husband this morning by the FBI?"

"Illuminate this," she screamed into the phone,

then she slammed it onto the receiver. She turned to get her car keys, but the phone rang again. "Are you a reporter?" she asked coldly.

"Ma'am, this is Sergeant Mayweather with the Charleston Police Department. I regret to inform you that your husband was taken into custody this morning by the Federal Bureau of Investigation. He's being held at our Mercer Street station. We thought you might like to visit with him before he's arraigned this afternoon. The arraignment is scheduled for three."

Audrey's face turned to stone. Her mind raced with possibilities awash with social embarrassment. "Oh God, what has he done?"

"Ma'am, the chief suggests you not speak with anyone until after you've seen your husband."

"Thank you, Officer. I'll be right down."

Chapter 17

Audrey Agosta hopped into her shiny green Volvo station wagon and pulled out of her garage as soon as the automatic opener had made enough room to scoot under the lip of the garage door. She was less than two blocks away when a van sporting the "WSAZ News Channel 3" logo passed her going in the opposite direction. "Bastards," she muttered as she screeched to a stop at a red light at the intersection of Kanawha Boulevard and Court Street.

When she arrived at the police station on Court Street, she pulled into a space reserved for judicial members only. *Why not?* she asked herself. *This is one of Michael's cars.* As she entered the station, a police officer who was leaving the building held the door open for her. She did not respond when he wished her a good afternoon. She just pushed down the corridor as though she owned it.

"I'm Mrs. Michael—" she said to the desk clerk.

"Yes, I know," the desk sergeant replied, cutting her off and pointing in the general direction she should go. "His Honor your husband is waiting for you in Holding Room C, just down the hallway, second door on the right."

"Thank you, Officer."

Audrey found Holding Room C and entered without knocking. Michael was reclining in a straight-back gray metal chair when she popped in. He smiled at her and wiped his nose with the back of his hand as she sat down across from him.

"You're disgusting," she said. "Use a damn tissue. Don't you know they're watching everything you do when you're shut away in this room like some common criminal? Show some decorum, Michael."

He showed her his wrists, bound together in traditional metal handcuffs. "Sorry. This *is* an uncommon situation and I guess I'm not thinking straight."

Audrey leaned over to Michael and gave him a brief peck on the lips. "So, what have you done to embarrass me in this way? I've already had calls from two reporters."

"I'm accused of rape."

Audrey looked surprised. "Rape? Who's charged you? It isn't one of our friends, is it?"

"You know better than that. It's a girl I knew in New York, back when I was seventeen and she was sixteen."

"Oh my God. You'd think there was some sort of time limit on such accusations." Audrey rubbed her forehead with the palm of her right hand. "When this hits the papers, they'll make me take a leave of absence from the middle school. Nobody's going to want their child in my classroom." She sighed and her eyes watered. "This is the end of my career."

"Nonsense. This is the end of *my* career, not yours. You may face some embarrassment, but I'll be disbarred. The only place I'll be able to get a job will be in some warehouse where people won't see me."

"So, are you guilty? Did you really rape that girl?"

"No, of course not. The problem is it's her word against mine."

"Well, a man of your position will sway a lot of public opinion against her."

"There's more, though. Do you remember the DNA test I took at Charlotte's request?"

"Yes. I remember telling you it wasn't a good idea."

"Well, I should have listened to you. The test identified me as the father of that girl's dead baby."

"Oh God," Audrey groaned.

"Those were my first words. The DNA from the baby's bones linked me to having had sex with her."

"Did you have sex with her?"

"Sure, lots of times. We were 'F-friends.' Do you know what that means?"

"Yes, of course. I'm an educator. But I don't think kids do that anymore."

"I'll bet many still do. Back then, she and I were among the vanguard. We read about it when it was a new thing and decided to become good at sex by learning with each other. We were kind of like lab partners."

Audrey thought for a moment. "That explains how good you were when I met you. You'd certainly had plenty of experience, more than I ever had, and I was four years older than you."

"Yeah, that experimental relationship made me better than average in bed, but I never knew it had made me a father. If I had, I would have been mortified."

Audrey sighed. "So, Your Honor, what's next, other than the press having a heyday over our dilemma?"

"I'll be arraigned within the hour and then they'll ship me to New York, where I'll stay in jail until they set bail in a separate arraignment. You can bet bail will be high because I'm a non-resident and, in their minds, I'll be a flight risk."

"Do you think we have enough savings to pay your bail?"

"Maybe enough to arrange for it with a bondsman. We may have to sell off a few stocks. We'll have to see. A bigger concern right now is how the County will handle my situation. I'm betting they'll suspend me without pay until this thing blows over. We'll probably have to refinance our home and sell one of our cars just to keep food on the table. Then, of course, if you decide to stay in New York with me, we'll have to figure out how to pay for your apartment or hotel room."

"And what about Charlotte's wedding? Will you be able to walk her down the aisle, or will we have to postpone it?"

"If I'm out on bail, I'll have to get permission to leave the State of New York. Of course, my arrest may cause Peter and Charlotte enough embarrassment to call off the wedding...or at least to postpone it." Michael laughed for a moment and then finished it with a sigh. "You know I think they're too young to get married, but I certainly didn't plan to stop them by doing this."

****

Audrey called Jake Lomax, the husband of her bridge partner, and asked him if he would serve as her attorney, should she need one. He agreed and suggested she drive to his office. He would accompany her home and arrange for the Charleston Police Department to station a couple of men and a squad car in her driveway to fend off nosey reporters.

When Jake and Audrey arrived at her home, four carloads of reporters and one digital video van were waiting for them. The van was parked across the entrance to her driveway, so Jake told Audrey to drive across her lawn and into her garage. She honked her horn and sent reporters scattering when she did.

Once inside, Audrey closed the garage door before she and Jake got out of her Volvo and entered her kitchen.

"They're going to be a pain in your ass for the next few days, Audrey," Jake said, running his fingers through the sides of his salt and pepper hair.

She plopped her purse on the pink granite kitchen counter. "Yes, I know. I'm taking my phone off the hook and having all my friends call me on my cell phone."

Jake pulled his cell phone out of his gray pinstriped suit coat and called his secretary for a ride back to his office. "Wait outside for me," he said. "I won't leave the house until the police are here."

He turned to Audrey. "Now listen carefully to me…"

The cabinets in the Agosta's kitchen were dark cherry. Audrey pulled a tumbler from an upper cabinet, poured a glass of pinot noir, and motioned to see if Jake wanted a glass.

"I'm serious," he said. "You have a few things to do before you scamper off to New York."

Audrey drank an entire glass of wine and then poured herself another. "Okay, Daddy, you have my full attention."

"You need to be sure your mortgage payment is

made."

"It's on autopayment at the bank."

"Good. Be sure you have enough in the account to cover it for a couple of months. Also, you need to be sure your mail is held or else you need to get somebody to pick it up for you every day until you get back."

Audrey swallowed a mouthful of wine. "Will do."

"Do you have an alarm system that notifies the police if there's a break-in?"

"Yes."

"Good. Be sure it's armed before you leave…and go to the bank and clear your credit cards, just in case you need the cash for an extended visit."

"Okay, I'll try to remember all that. She pulled her cell phone from her purse and waved it in the air. "You have my number on yours for speed dial?"

"Yes, and you have mine, so we can be in constant communication. I'll keep things as quiet as I can around here. Does Michael have an attorney?"

"No, I think he's waiting to hire one in New York. Do you have any recommendations?"

"He'll need a top-drawer trial attorney with lots of experience. I'll call around and see what I can find out. Maybe I can get him a short list of savages and text it to you. Meanwhile, you have a safe trip."

Chapter 18

I took a break from calling people who had been in high school with Margo Borst and Michael Agosta, and I decided, instead, to research New York State laws pertaining to the burial of the dead. Somewhere in the laws had to be a violation I could give to the D.A. to hang on Margo Borst. But there seemed to be nothing.

I called the County Clerk's office and asked to speak with whomever could answer questions about burial laws. I was directed to Lorraine Fuchs, a pleasant and knowledgeable voice on the other end of the line.

"I'm afraid the most severe penalty you're going to find is going to be a slap on the wrist or perhaps a small fine for not following local protocol," she said.

I picked up a pen and readied myself to jot down a few notes. "Like what? Can you give me an example?"

Mrs. Fuchs answered matter-of-factly. "Well, it's against State law to bury a cadaver without a medical examiner's affidavit of death."

"What's the penalty?"

"That probably would be up to the County court. I think the State courts wouldn't want to waste their time with such a small infraction and they'd send it down to the County level. Where was the body buried again?"

"In the basement of a house."

"Well, there again I think it's just a minor infraction. Just a minute Mr. Jones." She rattled the phone and breathed heavily into the receiver while she looked something up.

"You still there?"

"Yes, ma'am."

"It's right here." She summarized what she was reading. "You can bury a body on your own property, but you must draw a map of the property showing the burial ground. Then you're required to file it with the property deed so the location will be clear to others in the future." She paused for a moment. When she did, I could hear her breathing again. "Hmmm. Oh yes, there also is a statute requiring the burial ground to be at least sixteen hundred and fifty feet from any dwelling."

"If you don't do all that, how much is the fine?"

"That would be up to the County Clerk. If I were to guess…" She started calculating in her head. "…the cost to file a revised deed is a hundred and fifty dollars. Failure to file it properly usually adds another thirty-five dollars to the cost."

"Not much for violating the law. A parking ticket is more than that." I thought for a moment. "Wait. Did you say sixteen hundred feet? There's a cemetery less than two hundred feet from the house where the body was found."

"This statute only applies to private cemeteries. I'll bet you're talking about a public cemetery or a church cemetery. They're both exempt."

"Anything about failure to report a death?"

"Well, normally when a person dies, the next of kin calls the police and the police call an undertaker. If the death is caused by anything other than natural causes, public health law requires the police to refer the case to the county coroner or the medical examiner. They then examine the body for cause of death and fill out the necessary medical certification so the body can be disposed of properly."

"So, what you're telling me is if I dig up a skeleton in my back yard, it's no big deal?"

"Well, Mr. Jones, if it's a Native American burial ground, you might have a problem. Otherwise, you might have to pay to have the skeleton formally exhumed and relocated to a cemetery of your choice at your own expense."

"Jesus…" I hung up the phone in frustration.

****

The process of moving Michael from West Virginia to New York was complicated. First, the D.A. in Willow Falls had to draft a letter to the governor of the State of West Virginia to be signed by the governor of New York State requesting Michael's extradition. That process required a full two weeks to move through the pile of papers which both governors had to review each day. Then, an extradition hearing had to be scheduled in West Virginia. However, certain of his own innocence and wanting to clear his name before the election, Michael waived his right to an extradition hearing. West Virginia then notified New York State that Michael was ready for transfer. New York sent two state troopers, who drove roundtrip at taxpayers' expense to bring Michael to Willow Falls for arraignment.

Once in Willow Falls, Michael was turned over to the local police, who fingerprinted him again and then took him before a judge for a bail hearing. Asked if he had an attorney or would like one appointed by the court, Michael told the judge he did not yet have an attorney, but he hoped to have one within a day. Satisfied that Michael was an atypical criminal, the judge set his bail at only one hundred thousand dollars, and Michael was locked in a jail cell at the police headquarters until bail could be arranged.

The next afternoon, Audrey arrived at the Willow Falls police station with Michael's attorney, a gentleman named Lester Brockbank, who had a sterling reputation as a trial lawyer and who had come highly recommended by one of Jake Lomax's New York contacts. After listening to Audrey's plea for assistance and after accepting a sizeable deposit for his services, Brockbank agreed to serve as Michael's attorney. Then, before lunch at Audrey's expense, Brockbank helped her secure the necessary bail money through a local bondsman.

Michael was released on the recognizance of his attorney, and then he, Brockbank, and Audrey returned to her hotel suite, where they discussed the case. After Michael described his high school relationship with Margo and professed his innocence of the rape charge, Brockbank told Michael he did not think the district attorney had much to go on.

"Basically, it's your word against hers," Brockbank said.

"Well, this *is* the age of the 'Me Too' movement," Michael replied, "so female jurors are likely to side with the supposed victim regardless of the lack of evidence."

"A witness to corroborate your alibi would be helpful. Back in high school, did you tell anyone about your FF arrangement?"

Michael shook his head. "No. I tried to honor

Margo's request that as friends we would protect each other from rumors and gossip."

"How about later…maybe in college?"

"No, not even then. She was my friend, not some kind of conquest. Besides, once I left Willow Falls, I was making friends and dating girls in high school in Ohio. Then, college in West Virginia separated me even further from memories of Margo. She just became an unimportant someone from my past. Someone who I really didn't think about too often."

Chapter 19

Lance Freeborn called Margo and asked to meet with her in his office. "Let's do it tomorrow, and don't bring Henry," he said. "We need to get down to some important business, and his emotional outbursts simply aren't helpful."

After Henry left for work the next day, Margo took a shower and dressed in a conservative blue plaid pant suit for her meeting. Her hair style was five years behind the times, and her make-up was basic.

She arrived at Lance's office a few minutes before her ten o'clock appointment and, after pleasantries with Lance's secretary, waited patiently for her turn with her attorney. After a few minutes, a man she had seen somewhere before came out of Lance's office, nodded to her, and left quickly.

"Send Mrs. Lumpas in," Lance shouted from his office. His secretary looked up to tell Margo it was her turn, but Margo was already on her feet and tugging at the legs of her pant suit. She smiled at Lance's secretary and then walked into his office.

"Who was that man?" Margo asked as she sat down in a tufted button leather chair across the desk from Lance.

"Gazette reporter."

Margo felt a shot of adrenalin shoot through her chest. "He wasn't looking for information about my case, was he?"

"I'm afraid so. He's got the police beat."

She slumped in her chair. "Oh God. It begins…"

"Yes, it does." Lance loosened his tie and released the top button. "He read the police blotter this morning and saw that Michael Agosta was arraigned for rape yesterday. He also saw that you're the plaintiff and I'm the attorney representing you." Lance opened a rectangular wooden box and offered Margo a cigarette. She shook her head. He took one for himself and lit it with a Bic lighter bearing a New York Yankees logo. "Didn't take long, did it?"

Margo shook her head again. Her face was stressed, and her neck was splattered with red blotches.

"It's gonna hit the paper tomorrow, so you'd better prepare Henry. He's certainly going to be approached for a comment by follow-up reporters, probably the media, too—radio and TV. And you'd better prepare yourself, as well. I'll help you with that."

"My quiet little world is going to explode, Lance. How can I protect my children from the questions their friends will ask?"

"Worse than the questions will be the accusations and name calling. Children can be brutal that way."

Margo nodded her head. She wiped tears from her watery eyes.

"I need you to help me prepare the District Attorney's case," Lance said. "The more evidence we can acquire, the faster we can complete the trial and send this bastard to jail."

She dropped both hands into her lap. "I'm not sure how I can help you."

Lance began by having Margo go over the details

of her "year in Hell," when Michael was raping her on a weekly basis under the threat of personal and social destruction by lies. She offered nothing he had not heard before.

Lance twirled his pencil in the air. "I still find it difficult to believe anyone would suffer such abuse for so long a time without telling someone. The defense attorneys will use that against you to show that perhaps you were a willing participant."

Margo's eyes watered again, and she wiped them dry. She knew her excuse was lame. How could she ever convince a jury, especially when it was not even the truth?

"Didn't you confide in anyone…your sister? Your mother? Your priest?"

Margo shook her head. "No. I was afraid."

Lance plopped his notebook onto his desk. "Your behaviors back then were not like human nature as I know it, Margo. It's all very unnatural for a person not to fight back in some way."

Margo raised her hands as though she were pleading. "You have to understand I was not a popular girl. I wasn't pretty. I didn't date, didn't play any sports, and wasn't involved in after school activities of any sort. I was even afraid to hang with the druggies and the goths."

Lance shook his head slowly. "You don't paint a picture of a confident young girl, not one whom most parents would raise."

"I was only sixteen and knew almost nothing of boy-girl relationships when it first happened. Michael was a year older, and I was enthralled to have a boy take interest in me, especially one who was older than I was. I thought he really liked me. But all he wanted was to put a notch on his belt."

"But when you figured that out, why didn't you seek help?"

"I wanted to, but he threatened me repeatedly. I was naive and lacked the confidence to do that. Who would believe me? I was the timid little mouse, and he was the big ugly rat."

Lance picked up his notebook and jotted a few lines. "I like your analogy. Maybe I can weave it into the D.A.'s opening statement…you know, create an image which the jury can't shake."

Margo sighed and nodded.

"You have to help me, Margo. I need more. If you can think of anything, even something you think is insignificant, you give me a call or email me. Okay?"

The meeting was over, and more quickly than Margo had thought it would be. She nodded, rose, and walked out of Lance's office.

****

Lance Freeborn arrived on time for his late afternoon meeting with the District Attorney. When he entered Charles Claiborne's office, I was already seated.

"Good. Glad you're here, Lance. You know Bart Jones, don't you?"

Lance nodded and offered me his hand. I rose from my steel and black vinyl chair to shake Lance's hand. Then we both sat down.

Claiborne walked behind his desk and plopped uncomfortably into a tired high back chair. He was a tall man with broad shoulders and massive hands that extended from his shirt cuffs like spades. And he appeared troubled. "Gentlemen, we've got a bit of a predicament before us with this rape case."

I nodded, awaiting description of the problem. Lance Freeborn simply stared at the D.A. like a deer caught in headlights.

"All we got is the plaintiff's accusation, a set of twenty-five-year-old bones that are as clean as if my ex-wife's cat had been licking them, and a DNA analysis that points a finger at two people as the parents of the bones."

"It may be enough to convince the jury of rape," Lance said.

"Maybe back when you first started practicing, but not anymore. We need motive and some sort of corroboration of the rape."

Lance sat forward in his chair. "He was seventeen and horny. She was sixteen and vulnerable. That's all the motive you need to point to a probable rape, especially with a dead child as evidence of penetration. My client admits the child was hers."

I leaned forward. "So far, I haven't found anyone who really knew Mrs. Lumpas when she was in Willow Falls High School, Charlie. She was just there, an invisible face in the crowd. Most don't remember her at all, even when I show them her yearbook photo."

"How about her sister?" Claiborne asked.

"Since she learned of Mrs. Lumpas' case, she's gone missing. Probably wants to avoid her neighbors and maybe the publicity that's coming. Maybe she's gone down to the Bronx, or she's left the state. None of her neighbors seem to know…or care, for that matter. But I'll keep trying to locate her."

"And I've been working with Mrs. Lumpas,"

Freeborn said, "trying to get her to remember who she might have told about the rapes. So far, her memory banks are as empty as if the rapes never happened. But I'll keep working on her. I may employ a hypnotist…"

The D.A. raised one eyebrow, shook his head slowly, and moved his pointer finger back and forth.

"…not as a witness, but as someone who might help her remember something we can use."

"What about the defendant?" Claiborne asked, turning his attention to me. "You got anyone who knows something? You know how we boys used to brag about our conquests back when we were seventeen. That's what made girls popular. Some of them couldn't get a date if they didn't put out before midnight."

I never bragged about my own high school conquests. But then, I did not have any to brag about. Yet now I knew the D.A. had been active in high school. Well, at least the D.A. was bragging indirectly about being sexually active as a kid.

I shook my head. "Thus far, I've interviewed only three boys in the Class of Two Thousand who still live locally, and none of them remembers Agosta. He wasn't there during their senior year, and like Mrs. Lumpas, he wasn't in the in-crowd when he attended high school in Willow Falls."

The D.A. put both hands on his desk. "You boys have to help me, you hear? I've got a judge from West Virginia awaiting trial here on a rape charge which we can't prosecute without better evidence. I should have waited to charge and extradite him." The D.A. wiped his brow with a handkerchief. "Meanwhile, he's a candidate for the West 'by God' Virginia State

Supreme Court of Appeals and he's likely to sue us for false arrest and defamation of character if we release him for lack of evidence. Willow Falls can't afford something like that. Hell, if we get sued, I'll lose my job."

Chapter 20

Michael and Audrey were in their motel room when Audrey's cell phone rang. It was Jake Lomax, her attorney.

"Well, the damn papers have Michael's face spread all over them this morning with the word 'rapist' bigger than their damn banners. Audrey, you can expect some backlash from this."

"I called my principal before I left for New York. I'm sure he's told the superintendent by now."

"No, I mean from your friends and from the social clubs you're in. You can bet your bottom dollar all those sweet faces who approach you with sympathy are just drooling at the opportunity to learn something they can spread around on top of the other dirt. You be careful with what you say to anybody, okay?"

Audrey dug the fingertips of both hands into her forehead. "Oh, Jake, you make it sound so miserable."

"It's human nature, that's all." Lomax cleared his throat. "Is Michael there?"

"Yes. We're just sitting here waiting until we hear from the County Court to tell us when we'll go to trial."

"Have you heard from Michael's attorney today?"

"His name is Lester Brockbank. He's a nice man. Seems very thorough."

"Well, you'd better put your phone on 'speaker' so Michael can hear what I'm going to tell you."

Audrey did not like the tone of Jake's voice. She turned the television off and had Michael join her at the small round table near the balcony of their hotel room. "Okay, Jake, you're on speaker. Michael's here, too."

"Good. Michael, I don't have good news for you. You may hear this from your New York attorney, but I thought you should hear it from me, first."

"Go ahead, Jake. I'm prepared for just about anything right now," Michael replied.

"So, I've learned the County is pulling you off the bench."

"Well, I expected that. It should be a temporary thing until I get back."

Audrey had a look of horror on her face. Michael patted the back of her hand.

Lomax continued, "Well, they're not talking temporary down here. Your name plate has already been removed from your office and Cynthia Plummer has replaced you."

"The wife of the County Manager?"

"Yes."

"That's nepotism. It smacks of collusion and corruption. Follow the money, Jake. And see who's on the docket of upcoming cases. There's something bigger going on. Somebody's paid Plummer to get a free ride on what should be a heavy jail sentence."

"I agree, and I'll keep an eye on it. But it gets worse, Michael…"

Michael slumped his shoulders. "Aw jeez."

"The Republicans have asked the State Election Commission to remove your name from the ballot for State Supreme Court of Appeals. They want you replaced with Christine Massullo. They think she still has a chance to beat the Democrat, even though the election is only four weeks away."

Jake Lomax's news sent Michael into an emotional spiral. He could see both his personal and professional lives spiraling hand-in-hand down the tube. Everything he had worked for was being destroyed by a single unproven accusation brought forward by a forgettable girl from his past. A girl who meant nothing then and who should mean nothing now. Except she held his life and his reputation in her hands. If they could just talk, maybe he could put this whole thing to bed and reclaim his life in West Virginia.

****

At eleven in the morning, Charlotte called, crying and sobbing. "My DNA test came back this morning."

Audrey held her breath, then asked the anticipated question. "Do you have the marker for Childhood Alzheimer's?"

"No, but…"

"Thank God," Audrey whispered.

"But Peter's parents read the paper today and think we need to call off the wedding. They're embarrassed by all the negative press and think having Daddy at the ceremony and reception will cast dispersion upon their family. They don't even answer their phone anymore."

"You just go over there and tell Peter's parents this is a ploy by the Democrat Party to keep your daddy off the bench of the Court of Appeals. You tell them it's just like what happened to Kavanaugh."

"They're Democrats, Ma. They're glad something like this has happened to a Republican nominee for the judgeship. They just wish it didn't involve Daddy because it's embarrassed their family. Peter told me I ought to stay away from them for a few days. He's planning to sleep over with his parents for the rest of the week and then he says we'll have to discuss what to do about the wedding."

"I'm sorry, darling, but I can't control how people like Peter and his parents react to this kind of news. But you must believe in your Daddy. He didn't rape anyone, and I'm certain he'll be exonerated and this whole thing will blow over."

Audrey hung up the phone and turned to Michael, who was leaning back in his chair, staring at the ceiling as he listened to one side of the conversation. "I guess you heard. Charlotte's a mess. Her wedding might be off because Peter's parents are highly embarrassed. I guess she and Peter are quarreling and have split up for the time being."

"Is there any good news at all?" Michael asked.

"Yeah. She got her DNA results. She doesn't have the Childhood Alzheimer's marker."

Chapter 21

Redoubling my efforts, I returned to my office, where I reviewed the list of women who had graduated in the Willow Falls High School class of 2000 and who still lived locally. I had only checked off three names thus far and realized I needed to get on the stick if I planned to help Charlie prosecute the case. Starting with the next name on my list, I picked up the phone and dialed the home of Darlene Williams Smith. She picked up after only two rings.

"Yeah?" she asked unenthusiastically.

I introduced myself and explained the nature of my call.

"Yeah, I remember her. We were in homeroom together." I could hear her running the water in her sink. "Listen, Margo's only friend in high school, if you could call her that, was a drip named Zeena something or other. She would sit with Margo at lunch whenever she was between boyfriends. I wouldn't call her a close friend. Maybe a friend of convenience, if you know what I mean."

When we hung up, I looked in the yearbook and found her—Zeena Zumwalt. She was a plain girl whose senior picture showed some zits around her mouth and on her forehead. Today, such photographic blemishes would have been erased magically by technology. I checked the telephone directory, but there were no

Zumwalts still living in Willow Falls, so I opened the list of alumni given to me by Elise Grogan, the Assistant Superintendent of Schools. Bingo! Zeena was married and living in Syracuse as Zeena Schwartz.

I called her. "Mrs. Schwartz, my name is Detective Bartholomew Jones of the Willow Falls Police Department. I'm investigating a case, and your name was given to me as a person who might be able to help me make heads or tails out of a few details."

"Just call me Zeena," she replied. "I've been divorced for six months now, and I'd like to drop the creep's last name, if you know what I mean."

"Sure, Zeena." I thought about what to ask next and decided an in-person interview might be best. "Do you remember Margo Borst from high school?"

"Yeah. I heard she got married, but I don't know her married name, if that's what you're looking for."

"It's Lumpas, Margo Lumpas."

There was a pause on Zeena's end of the line. "I did better with last names, not that Schwartz is anything to write home about, but at least I climbed up the alphabet. Back in high school I was always seated in the back row in class because my last name started with a 'Z.' The letter 'S' is at least seven letters closer to the beginning of the alphabet. Margo must have gone from the front of the classroom to the middle somewhere."

I waited patiently until Zeena stopped babbling. "I'd like to chat with you about Margo, if that would be okay with you."

The tone of Zeena's voice changed to concern. "Has she done something wrong? I mean, she didn't seem like the type who'd shoplift or anything like that."

"No, she's not a shoplifter." I drummed my fingers

on my desk. "Is there someplace in Syracuse where we could meet to chat a bit about Margo?"

"Yeah. How about the Dinosaur Barbecuc? The food's good and the atmosphere is great."

I had heard of the famous Dinosaur Barbecue from the guys in the police department, but had never had the occasion to go there, so I agreed. We set Saturday at seven in the evening as the meeting time. Zeena would get a table and keep an eye out for me. I would be wearing a New England Patriots cap.

****

On Saturday at five, I hopped into my car and followed the New York State Thruway to Syracuse. My cell phone's GPS guided me to Willow Street, where only one building was lit up. And it was hopping. It was a two-story red brick building with the words *Dinosaur Bar-B-Que* tattooed on the edge of a balcony where at least fifty people were partying, beers in hand. I searched for a few minutes before finding a parking space three blocks away, and then I walked back along the uneven sidewalk to the entrance. The last portion of the block was reserved for motorcycles, and more than thirty were lined up, serving as a reminder that the Dinosaur once had been a bikers' bar, but was now full of yuppies.

I pushed open the door and waded into a sea of bodies, all crammed together. Some of the men wore biker's vests, others wore suits and ties, and yet others simply wore jeans and tee shirts. College girls wore sorority jackets or sweaters, working class girls wore tee shirts and were braless, and the wives and girlfriends of the men in suits wore nice dresses and pantsuits. Most drank beer in a variety of colors. Some held wine glasses. Mounted above the fray, the heads of wild boar, bears, and antlered animals of several species watched the unnatural mixture of human subclasses awkwardly intermingling. Posters and pictures of the famous were everywhere. Barmaids carrying small trays of beers begged their way from the bar to the tables they were serving. It was a madhouse, and I now understood why the guys back at the station loved the Dinosaur so much.

For a place with a seating capacity of seventy-five, the Dinosaur was bursting with three or four times more people than it could legally handle. I wondered how Zeena Schwartz would ever find me, especially since at least eight men were wearing Patriots caps. But before I could determine a strategy to find Zeena, a barmaid tapped me on the shoulder. She was tattooed with a multicolored jungle scene from her ears down to her fingertips on both arms. Her black hair was pulled back into a ponytail. "Are you Jones?" she asked.

"Yeah. Are you Zeena?"

"No." She pointed over her shoulder to a raised booth in the corner. I looked. A woman with red hair and a bright yellow blouse was waving at me.

"That's Zeena."

"Thank you." I pushed through the crowd toward Zeena.

"Hey, Jones," the barmaid shouted, "what'll you be drinking?"

"How about a draft brown ale?"

"You got it."

"And bring another of whatever Zeena is drinking"

"Okay…"

The barmaid turned toward the bar and melted into

the crowd.

When I got to the booth, I offered my hand to Zeena, and she spoke first. "You were the only one dressed like a nerd. Had to be you."

She had already downed two pints of beer, and her eyes glowed with the light of a slight alcoholic high. I suspected the red of her hair was a rinse which brought her natural mousy brown color to life.

"Have you ordered?" I asked.

She handed me a menu, and I saw she was still wearing her wedding ring. She noticed my gaze. "It's a good way to pick up guys. The ring says you're spoken for, and there's no question of whether you're looking for commitment. It's just a quickie in the back of a car or in somebody's apartment, and then you're free to go home to whatever's waiting for you."

I nodded and looked at the menu. The barmaid was on us quickly. "Gimme the Carolina pulled pork sandwich with slaw," I said. Zeena ordered the West Texas Rib-eye. I could tell it was going to be an expensive night.

"This place is crazy with people," I said, breaking the ice.

Zeena nodded. "Half of Syracuse comes here over the three-night weekend. Fridays and Saturdays it's mostly younger people. Sundays is when the married couples and families come."

When dinner arrived, I sprinkled some hot sauce on my pulled pork sandwich and took a bite. It was mean with smokey flavor. "So, tell me about Margo."

Zeena finished chewing a chunk of steak and downed it with a swallow of stout. "Margo and I were friends." She paused for a moment. "Let me rephrase that…I was the closest thing to a friend that Margo had." She cut another piece of steak and shoveled it into her mouth. "Margo was essentially a loner," she said, still chewing.

"What about boyfriends? Did she have any?"

She sprinkled some salt on the fries which were piled beside her steak, and then she smothered them in ketchup. "None that I know of. I mean, she never mentioned one."

"Not even an FF?"

She looked at me strangely, as if I had used a term she hadn't heard in a long time. Maybe since high school. "Funny you should mention that. I remember one time she talked to me about how I should get an FF. She said it sounded like a good thing."

Zeena stuck a few fries in her mouth, leaving a smear of ketchup on her upper lip. She wiped it off with her napkin. "Margo said she had been thinking about doing it, herself…becoming an FF…and she said she had a guy she thought might be interested."

Zeena swallowed some more beer. "She thought I should pick some safe guy and get into that kind of an arrangement with him."

I cocked my head. "Did you?"

"Nope. I had lots of different boyfriends back then and didn't need that kind of experience because I already had it, if you know what I mean. I was thirteen the first time…but almost fourteen."

"Who was the guy she thought might be interested in an FF relationship?"

"Don't know." Zeena stuffed another piece of steak into her mouth.

I pulled a list of names from my pocket. "Can I

read you a few names and see if anyone rings a bell?"

"No. I told you she never told me who it was...probably a nerd of some kind. The cool guys had enough opportunities with the popular girls. They didn't need a steady with no commitments. They had anybody they wanted with no commitments. It was that way with the cool girls, too."

I was finishing my sandwich when a large, shirtless man wearing a biker vest tapped my shoulder. "Would you two mind if me and my old lady share your booth? She's tired of being jostled by the crowd."

"If you hang around close and don't mind waiting, we'll be done in five minutes," I replied.

The behemoth stepped away and whispered into his woman's ear. She looked at the booth and nodded.

I signaled to the barmaid, who brought me the check. I handed her a credit card and she pushed through the crowd to process it. Then I turned back to Zeena. "Would you be willing to tell a jury everything you just told me? It would mean a trip to Willow Falls."

"Sure, if you'll pay me for my testimony and cover my meals and travel expenses. Haven't been to Willow Falls in a nun's age."

When the waitress returned, she handed me a standard leatherette bill holder. I signed the Dinosaur's copy, pocketed my receipt and credit card, and left fifteen dollars cash on the table for the barmaid.

As Zeena and I were leaving, I looked back and saw two large men and two women squeeze into the empty booth. One of the men stuffed the fifteen-dollar tip into his vest pocket. I mentioned it to the bouncer and pointed the guy out. Then Zeena and I beat it out of the Dinosaur to avoid the fight.

Chapter 22

When her phone rang, Audrey answered it without looking to see who was calling. "Audrey here."

"Good afternoon, Audrey." It was her attorney, Jake Lomax. "Is Michael there with you?"

"Yes. Where else would we be? We never leave this room except to walk the hallways to reduce our stress."

"Well, please tell him I'm working on his behalf back here at home. I've filed suit against the Republican Party for taking action against Michael prior to his being found guilty of the charges in New York."

"Thanks, Jake. Isn't that supposed to be the American way…innocent until proven guilty?"

"Not necessarily, Audrey. The newspapers are controlled by the Democrats, and they already have him convicted before his trial date has been set."

"Bastards." Audrey knew the papers leaned heavily toward the left and had heard Michael rant about how real journalism died in the seventies. Michael claimed large conglomerates, funded by George Soros, now owned the papers and their agenda was always anti-Republican and anti-Conservative. Audrey was not sure if that was true, but at the moment, every journalistic piece written about Michael was negative. The press was grinding his name into the mud.

"I've also launched a lawsuit against Albany County, New York, for defamation of character," Jake said. "We can easily trace Michael's removal from the West Virginia ballot to the charges brought against him by Albany County. If he is found innocent of the charges, I think we can recover all his lost wages and some of his prestige."

"Thanks, Jake. We'll keep you up to speed on what's happening here."

"I know you will, Audrey, and so will Les Brockbank."

****

Margo pulled the family's copper-brown minivan into the garage of their Cape Cod home and carried a package of chopped meat and an onion into the kitchen. "I'm home." She called out.

Henry walked into the kitchen. "Let's order out."

"I promised the kids spaghetti tonight."

"I took them over to my sister's while you were out. She's going to take them to the new Disney flick and then out for burgers."

Margo's face dropped. "Oh, I didn't know you were going to do that. I wish you had told me, so I wouldn't have bought the meat until tomorrow."

Henry opened the refrigerator and put the package of ground beef onto the bottom shelf. "I just need some time with you."

Margo looked up, unsure if he wanted sex or if he wanted to talk. She had been worried about their relationship ever since the police had questioned her about the bones. In fact, they had not made love since then. And it had been weeks.

Henry poured them both a glass of pinot grigio and

escorted her into the living room. He brought the bottle with him. When they were both seated on the sofa, Henry explained what was on his mind. "Lance called me this morning."

"Oh?"

Henry nodded. "He's worried they may not have enough evidence to pursue the rape case against Agosta."

Margo inhaled deeply and blew the air forcefully from her nostrils.

"He's hoping you've had time to remember more that will help him to build the case, especially the name of anyone you might have told about the rapes. He's wondering if maybe you've dreamed a recollection...dreams have a way of bringing up long-forgotten things, you know."

"I remember almost nothing." Margo took a large sip of her wine, almost emptying her glass. "I've spent the last twenty-five years trying to put it behind me...to forget the whole thing...and I guess I've done a pretty good job of it."

Henry finished his glass of wine in three swallows and refilled both glasses. "Lance has difficulty believing you never told me about it. In fact, I'm having the same difficulty. You know, I think you'd have wanted me to know about it, especially since it's a horror you've held onto since youth."

"Henry, if the baby's bones hadn't been dug up, I'd never have told you about it because it's a shameful thing, and it's so far in the past. Over the past twenty-five years I've worked through it all and didn't want it to cause ripples in our relationship...yours and mine." She downed half of her second glass of wine. "More than anything, I didn't want you to see me as a victim. I'm a different person now, not as weak as I was when I was sixteen."

Henry lied to support her self-image. "No, you're not weak at all now."

"If that bastard tried to rape me today, I'd rip his thing off, the way Lorena Bobbitt did."

Henry smiled and finished his second glass of wine, prompting Margo to do the same. He poured them both the remaining wine, emptying the last few drops into Margo's glass.

"Are you trying to get me drunk, Henry?"

He smiled again, then set the bottle on the table. "Do you have any other secrets, sweetheart?

She shook her head. She was not sure where this conversation was going. Henry usually was not so probing.

"Husbands and wives don't need to have any secrets between them, unless it's something they both know, and they're keeping it secret from somebody else."

Margo nodded. "Like last year when we borrowed your sister's car, and you scratched the bumper when you backed into the parked police car."

"Yes, that exactly," Henry said with a smile. "That's one of those little secrets which we should share only with ourselves."

"I promise you I have no other secrets, little or big, that I'm hiding from you."

Henry scooted over next to Margo and kissed her neck. "I love the way your neck smells."

Margo was enjoying Henry's advances, but she had one last thing to say. "If you ever discover that I have any other secrets from you, I hope you'll divorce me because I wouldn't be the type of wife you deserve."

Margo felt Henry's hand slide under her skirt. He breathed heavily on her neck. "You're the love of my life, sweetheart. What could you possibly do to cause me to divorce you?" He ran his tongue across her lips.

Margo lay down on the sofa, pulling Henry on top of her. And for the first time in more than a month, they made love. And on the living room sofa. The same sofa where they had conceived Zoe.

****

I tapped the red button on my cell phone, ending the call. After days of no luck in finding anyone who remembered Michael Agosta, I had just found two. One interviewee had been in physical education class with Michael and remembered him as a guy who had been somewhat quiet and shy at the beginning of their junior year, but by the end of the year, he had seemed more confident. He described Michael as "oozing a quiet confidence which was unnaturally mature for someone who was only seventeen years old."

The second guy seemed to know more details about Michael than the other, so I went to see him. Besides, the first guy lived an hour north in Saratoga Springs, while the second guy lived right in town. By two in the afternoon, I was sitting with the second guy, John Armbruster, in the back yard of his center hall colonial in a suburb of Willow Falls.

"So, what do you recall the most about Michael Agosta?" I asked.

Armbruster squirmed in his chair, as though what he was about to say was more subjective than concrete. "Agosta didn't seem interested in dating, as though he was either gay or he had something on the side he wasn't talking about."

"Can you give me more details or be more specific? Telling me that Agosta seemed gay isn't specific, unless Agosta, himself, told you he was gay or somebody who was gay told you he and Agosta were an item. You know what I mean?"

Armbruster nodded and took a quick swig of beer from a bottle of Corona. "So, one time during our junior year, I tried to get Agosta to ask my sister to the Junior Prom. I mean, she didn't have a date. But Michael wasn't interested, even though he knew my sister 'put out.' I mean…all the guys knew that."

"Why'd you pick Agosta instead of somebody else?"

"She pushed me to ask him because she thought he was cute, 'in a nerdish sort of way.' I mean, I wouldn't have picked him for her, but she did, and that's what she said. '…a nerdish sort of way.' But it didn't make a difference. He didn't seem interested in taking her to the prom or in screwing her… and that's what usually drove guys to go out with her…she put out."

"To your knowledge did Agosta date anybody?"

"To my knowledge, no. Not the entire year. That's why I thought maybe he was gay."

"Thanks for your help. If the case I'm working on goes to court, would you be willing to testify to everything you just said?"

"Sure. My sister doesn't live here anymore, so she won't care what's in the paper. What's this case about, anyway?"

"I'm not at liberty to say right now. But if you're called to testify, I'll let you know everything."

Chapter 23

I dialed Terry Moore, a former police officer who had changed careers and was now with the Department of Motor Vehicles in Albany. We were only acquaintances, but I felt comfortable making the call.

Moore's voice was familiar. "It's been a long time, Bart. How can I help you?"

I gave him a few details about the Agosta case and then got to the reason for my call. "I'm having difficulty locating the victim's sister. Thought maybe you had access to information which would help me track her down. Maybe social security number, federal tax records, or things like that."

"State Police might be a better starting point but give me what information you have, and I'll see what I can do."

I gave him her full name and her address in Willow Falls. Half an hour later, my cell phone rang. It was Terry Moore. "I got a few things." He gave me the social security number the DMV had on file for Darla Jayne Borst, a.k.a. Darla Jane Vasquez, and the credit card number she had used to renew her license plates back in April. "It's not much, but it may get you started. I still think you'd be better off letting the State Police help you locate her."

"Thanks, Terry. Next time you're in Willow Falls, I'll buy you a beer."

****

I ran her social security number, but Darla's address was still Willow Falls, and she wasn't working because she hadn't contributed anything to her Social Security account during the past quarter.

Then I contacted the Willow Falls National Bank and learned that Darla was a customer and had used her credit card at Verrigni's Quick Sack between eight and eight-fifteen on each of the past three mornings. They also emailed me a black and white photo of her face, taken during a recent transaction with a teller at the bank's downtown branch. She looked tired, perhaps overworked, in the picture.

I arrived at Verrigni's at seven forty-five the next morning, mixed a cup of half dark roast and half decaf, and sat in a booth near the front door with Darla's picture in my hand. Like clockwork, Darla walked into the Quick Sack at eight, and busied herself prepping two cups of coffee with cream and sugar.

I left my coffee at the booth and approached Darla from the side. She did not look too much like Margo. Her hair was salt and pepper instead of dark brown, her face bore deep lines, and her torso was thin. She carried her weight below her waist in a round rump and abdomen and large legs which made her jeans work like compressions socks.

"Darla?"

She looked up at me, then snapped plastic lids onto her two paper cups of coffee. "Am I supposed to know you?"

"My name is Bartholomew Jones. I'm with the Willow Falls Police Department and I'm trying to help your sister."

"She don't need no help. She got a rich husband." Darla scooped up her coffees and headed toward the cashier. I followed her. "Your sister is involved in a case I'm working on, and I'm hoping you can provide some information that will shed some light on it."

The cashier rang up Darla's coffees. "That'll be three dollars and twenty-three cents, honey."

While Darla set her cups on the counter and fumbled through her black leatherette purse for her credit card, I handed the cashier three dollars and twenty-five cents. When she gave me two pennies in return, I dropped them into the small cup used by random people who needed a few cents to pay their tab.

Darla picked up her coffees and headed toward the door.

"Please?" I pleaded. "I can always have you summoned into court."

Darla stopped and turned to look at me. "Now what kind of trouble would little Margo be in that would drag me into a courtroom?"

I invited Darla to sit in my booth for a few minutes. "Now don't take too long," she said. "Rolando don't like his coffee cold."

I asked if Darla had spoken to Margo lately. She hadn't seen her sister in almost a year. "She don't come to Willow Falls too often. She like to stay in that hoity toity Marshfield. Last time I went there, the cops pulled me over and told me I didn't belong. Told me to get back to Willow Falls."

I related the basic details about Margo's case—the rapes, the baby boy, the discovery of the bones. When I finished, Darla broke into a broad smile. "Woo hoo. Little Margo got herself into some shit, ain't she? I wish Mom and Pop were still around to see this. They probably rolling over in their graves."

I looked at Darla in disbelief. She sounded totally disconnected from her sister.

"Look," she continued, "Margo always thought she was better than me. She went and got herself that job in Marshfield and then she went to community college and then she got married to a teacher. She got it all. Me? I got pregnant in my senior year in high school and never been married. Raised two boys by myself. Now Rolando asked me to move in with him. He be a good man. Takes care of me. Never hits me. Don't want me working at Walmart no more."

I could see the hardships Darla had faced in life in the deep lines in her face and the callouses on her fingers. "Can you remember back in high school," I asked, "when Margo was a sophomore, and you were a senior? Do you remember a guy named Michael Agosta?"

Darla thought for a moment. "Naw. I hung with the Mexicans back then. Didn't mess with white guys."

"Can you remember anything about Margo back then? Did she ever confide in you that some guy was raping her?"

"Was she some guy's punch back then? Why that little…"

"Yeah, it doesn't seem like something she'd have let happen to her, does it?"

"She was always so reserved, like 'little miss perfect.' Her only problem was baby fat. If she would have stopped with the chips and chocolate bars, she'd have dropped a few pounds and the boys would have taken an interest in her. In her sophomore year she sort of chunked up, you know…" Darla paused. "Do you think maybe she chunked up back then because she was pregnant?"

"That could be one reason. It makes sense, doesn't it?"

Darla removed the top from one of the cups of coffee and took a sip. "So, what is it you want to know about Margo?"

"Did she ever confide in you about being raped?"

"Nope. This is the first time I'm hearing about it."

"Did she ever date anyone while you were still living home?"

"Like I said, she was a little chunky and she blew up a bit in her sophomore year. Not too many boys would have asked her out. Except…"

"Was there a boy?"

"Well, no…not exactly. But I do remember a couple of times when she threw her dirty clothes in the hamper in our bathroom. They smelled like…"

"Like what?"

"This is gonna sound stupid, but I remember thinking that her clothes…they smelled like sex."

"How exactly do you mean?

"Well, like female and male mixed together. I mean, I smelled it before on my own clothes after I was, well, intimate with my boyfriend. Her clothes smelled just like that."

"What did you do about it?"

Darla leaned back against the plastic of the booth's seat. "Like what? Tell our parents?" She smirked at me like I was from another planet. "I don't think so. I mean, when you were experimenting with sex, did you tell your parents?"

"You didn't talk with her about it…like a big sister helping her little sister through the maze of emotions that come with having sex?"

Darla snapped the plastic lid back onto her coffee cup. "Nope. If little Margo was experimenting, it was her business, not mine. And there was no way I was going to rat her out to our parents."

Darla had a point. And I nodded in agreement. What kid goes home and tells his parents the first time he has sex? Certainly, not me. And what kid tells his parents his brother or sister is having sex? It would be a breach of sibling trust. And the accusations can flow both directions.

Before Margo left Verrigni's, I gave her my business card and asked her to call if she remembered anything that might throw light on Margo's case. She gave me Rolando's home telephone number, where she could be reached during the workday. "Don't you be calling in the evening when Rolando's doing his business," she said. "He gets upset if another man is looking for me."

Chapter 24

I was at home, sitting at the kitchen table with a cup of coffee in my hand. I must have looked confounded.

"What's on your mind, Barty?" Rachel asked, returning to the kitchen table with a wet paper towel to brush away toast crumbs she had dropped when eating her light breakfast. "You seem really perplexed. Got a bad case?"

I took a sip of the black coffee Rachel had poured for me. "Why would you think that?"

"Oh, I've seen it before… that look on your face when you have a case which hands you twists and turns that don't make sense."

I blew across the top of my ceramic coffee mug and then took another sip. The brew was stronger than usual. "I'm dealing with a rape accusation, and it's not unlike Juanita Broderick or Paula Jones, except I have no corroboration. Nobody knows anything. The victim didn't tell anybody. The only thing I have is a baby, and the baby died at birth."

"Was the baby murdered?"

"At first, I thought so. But as the case has unraveled, I think the baby was dead or close to dead at birth, and the mother didn't have the necessary knowledge to save it. She wasn't even in a hospital, and she had no medical assistance of any kind."

"How horrible."

"Yeah, I hope the baby didn't suffer."

"No," Rachel said, "I mean how horrible for the mother. Delivering alone can't possibly be easy. They say Native American women would go off into the woods by themselves to have a baby, but I don't believe it. Other women are always there to help another woman deliver a child. In our modern society, no woman ever should have to deliver her baby alone. There's just no reason."

"How about a sixteen-year-old girl who's being raised by fundamentalist parents who don't know she's pregnant?"

"Hmmm," Rachel replied. "That paints a slightly different picture. You've added an element of anxiety and the fear of parental rejection and discipline."

"So, throwing in those elements, giving birth to a baby in an abandoned house isn't necessarily out of the question?"

"Being hidden away anywhere isn't out of the question, especially if your parents aren't supportive." Rachel stood and looked at herself in the oval mirror which hung on the wall beside our landline telephone. She touched up her oxblood lipstick. "Did you say it was a rape case?"

"Yes, that's what the victim claims."

"Horrible."

Rachel gave me a peck on the cheek. "I've got to go. Several patients are scheduled for MRI's this morning, and I need to have the machine ready to go before Dr. Patel arrives. See you this evening."

****

I was at my desk in the Willow Falls PD,

rummaging through a stack of papers related to Margo Lumpas when my phone rang. It was FBI Agent Casola. "What's up, Mona?" I asked.

"That's the same question I have for you."

"Too bad. I was hoping you were calling with more information for me. Maybe something that would wrap the BabyX case into a tidy package."

"Nope. Actually, I thought I'd better call you because my boss has ordered me to back off the case. He says it's out of our jurisdiction since no crimes appear to have been committed across state lines."

"Yeah, I figured that might happen. But thanks for what you and the Feds did for me. The two DNA work-ups have identified the probable parents, and I guess I can take it from here. Problem is there's very little corroboration to help the plaintiff. Most of the testimonies of her potential witnesses lend credence to the accused's story and not hers. Unless something breaks, he's gonna walk."

"A good-luck-wish is all I have to offer you, Jonesy. I'm off in another direction, myself."

"Like what?"

"Possible homicide that has been staged to look like suicide."

"Could prove interesting."

"Probably not. But remember that guy I told you about?"

"The private detective who dumped you after you told him you loved him?"

"Yeah, that's the one…Dan Arrow, the detective who's afraid of commitment."

"You didn't call him, did you?"

"Nope. He's called me to see if I can assist him

with the investigation."

"Be careful, Mona. If you get your expectations up too high, they may come crashing down on your head."

"Yeah. My sister Wendy told me the same thing. One thing's for certain…"

"What's that?"

"…I'm wearing three layers of clothes if I think there's the slightest chance I'm gonna be alone with him."

I wished Agent Casola well and then hung up the phone. The moment I did, my phone rang again. It was Charles Claiborne, the District Attorney.

"Yessir?" I said.

"Just a heads-up. The guy in the BabyX case has launched a defamation of character lawsuit against our County."

"Michael Agosta?"

"Yeah. Seems the Republican party of West Virginia has replaced him with another candidate for the State's Supreme Court of Appeals. He's blaming his arrest by New York for the loss of his candidacy, especially since all the polls had him ahead by more than fifteen points at the time of his arrest."

"Swell. I'm sure the County Manager is about ready to bite your head off."

"He's left me an angry message, but I haven't returned his call yet. I thought I'd call you first and get some good news about the investigation to pass along to him."

I rubbed my forehead with my free hand. "Listen, Chuck, so far all the plaintiff's potential witnesses can't corroborate her story. In fact, they tend to paint her as a willing participant in an FF relationship."

"You're shitting me…"

"I still have a few more people to interview. Can you hold off returning the call for a day or two?"

"Not likely. The County Board of Supervisors meets tomorrow night. The Manager's going to have to tell them about the pending lawsuit. This could cost the County millions of dollars. I'm going to have to call him tomorrow morning with an update on our investigation, so he has time to prepare."

I could hear the concern in the D.A.'s voice. "I'll try to finish my interviews today and draft a report for you. I'll try to have it to you by tomorrow morning. I'll call if it's going to be later."

"Good. And thank you for trying hard on this case. I hadn't anticipated its being such a loser. Like I said the other day, I should have waited to arrest Agosta. Bad call on my part."

The D.A. hung up before I could agree with him.

Chapter 25

I walked down to the second floor of the Willow Falls PD and knocked on Helen Martin's door.

"It's open," she called out.

I pushed the door open. "Hey, sweetheart, it's just me."

Helen was on her knees, her back turned toward the door, fishing for something under the small oak bookshelf behind her desk. She was wearing a sleeveless navy-blue dress with a white panel across the front.

"Whoa, is your dress a Michelle Obama knockoff?"

"Don't you come in here 'sweet-hearting' me, Jonesy. When you do, I know it means you got some mess you want me to clean up. Who'd you piss off this time?"

The D.A.'s got a gator on his butt and needs our help."

"So how come that old badger didn't call me himself?"

"Well, he asked me to dig up more evidence on the BabyX case and I'm the one who needs your help."

Helen stood up holding a ballpoint pen in her hand. "Well, that paints a different picture." She straightened her skirt. "Why didn't you just say so in the first place?"

"Well…"

"What do you need me to do?"

"You all finished with that suicide pact mess?"

"Yup, at least for the time being. Murder Case goes to trial next week."

"I've got a couple of peeps to interview, two males and two females."

"That's more than a couple. It's two couples."

I nodded at the obvious. "Yeah. You want the males or the females?"

"What am I looking for?"

"Anything that will help the D.A. press the case against the accused rapist."

"I'll take the females. If he did the same thing to one of them, they're more likely to talk to a female." Helen sat down and looked at the calendar on her computer screen. "How's about I do the interviewing the day after tomorrow?"

"Gotta be today. The D.A. wants the details put to bed by nine tomorrow morning. He has to report to the County Legislature tomorrow night."

"You got to give me half an hour to clean my calendar and then I'll come to your office for the names and addresses. You'd better remind me of all the particulars before I go and mess up by asking the wrong questions."

I went back to my desk and assembled the folders I had made for each of the four interviewees, including the basic questions I had asked all the others. When Helen arrived ten minutes later, I handed her folders for the two females and debriefed her on everything I knew about the case. One woman was known to sit at Margo Lumpas' table during lunch period. The other was the sister of a guy who was friends with Michael Agosta in their senior year in high school in Ohio. Both lived out of state, so Helen's interviews would be conducted by phone.

I was left with two names to interview, Pedro "Mescal" Herrera and Juaquin Mendez. I had no telephone numbers, but both men lived at the same address on Van Rensselaer Drive, a neighborhood which had been upper middle class back in the fifties, but which had slowly morphed into the slum it was today. I changed into plainclothes and checked that my .45 caliber SIG P220 was loaded and the safety was off before driving to their address.

As I passed 1362 Van Rensselaer on my left, I saw several Hispanic-outfitted Harleys parked in front. Three were full dressers with extra chrome, windshields, and multicolored plastic strips hanging from the ends of the handlebars. *Mexican Mafia or MS-13. I should have brought backup.*

But there was no time to waste, so I did a U-turn and parked beside a step van in front of the address. The building consisted of tired orange brick with patches of stucco and a rusted steel roof. The front door was simply a piece of plywood with a death's head painted in black at eye level. As I approached, I could hear laughter inside. Not knowing what else to do, I knocked.

"Wha' the fugg?" Somebody sounded annoyed.

When the door opened, I was greeted by the largest man I had ever seen in my life. With a square head and no neck, the man towered close to seven feet tall, and his waist was as large as a whiskey barrel. He was dressed in black denim sweatpants and a sweatshirt.

The toes of his black cowboy boots were embellished with razor sharp steel points. I could see a bulge at his waistline. *Probably a piece.*

"You wan' somethin' or you plannin' on dyin'?"

"I'm trying to locate Pedro Herrera or Juaquin Mendez. I'm hoping they can help me."

The giant turned. "Hey, Mescal, this hombre say he's lookin' for you."

A voice answered from somewhere in the back of the room. "Fine out if he tryin' to serve me."

The giant man turned back toward me.

"I heard him," I said. "Tell him I'm a police detective and I need his help to solve a case. It doesn't involve him, and I won't need him to testify."

Before the giant could relay the message, he was pulled aside by a middle-aged guy with a braided goatee and three gold upper teeth. He was wearing black Levi's and a blue cotton shirt. Only the top three buttons were fastened, exposing a triangular section of white tee shirt beneath. I assumed 'Mescal' was Pedro.

"Outside," Mescal instructed.

I obeyed, stepping back to the edge of the sidewalk. Mescal stepped out, his gold teeth reflecting the sun. He was followed by two others, all dressed the same: Black denim jeans and vests, white tee shirts, motorcycle boots, and gold chains. Lots of them.

Mescal seemed intrigued that a police detective would drop by without an invitation. "So whadda you wan', gringo?"

"I understand a girl named Darla Borst used to hang with you."

He cocked his head and stood with his feet separated at shoulder's width. "An' if she did?"

"I'm here about her younger sister, Margo. Do you remember her?"

He relaxed a little bit. "I might. Wha's the connection to me?"

"No connection to you. Do you know if Margo was raped by anybody?"

Mescal spit on the sidewalk and snickered. "L'il fat girl Margo? Nobody'd rape that."

The two men behind him laughed. They were at least twenty years younger than he was, so their laughter must have been situational—me, a gringo, at Mescal's mercy.

"She claims somebody did, and I'm trying to find corroborating evidence to that effect."

"Speak Eeenglish, man."

"I'm trying to find information that proves she was raped."

"Back when I was doing Puta-Dee…tha's what we call Darla back then…back when I was doing her, L'il Margo was gettin' it on wit' some white punk. Don't know his name."

"Really? What do you mean "getting it on'?"

"She was bangin' some little gringo kid about her age. They used a house over by the graveyard."

"An empty house?"

"Yeah. Nobody lived there."

"Was he raping her?"

Mescal smiled, his gold teeth shining in the sun. "No. She like it. You know wha' I mean?"

"How do you know this was happening?"

"This is our barrio, man. We got eyes everywhere. We know everything goin' on here."

"So, it wasn't rape?"

"Tha's wha' I said."

"Could I possibly interview Juaquin Mendez?

Mescal's face took on a look of sadness. "Can you speak with the dead? Juaquin ate a bullet in Troy two years ago."

"The stuff you told me…I don't suppose I could get you to testify in a courtroom or sign a deposition?"

He laughed and then gave me a serious stare. "Get out of here, hombre. You don't belong here. Don't come back, and don't send no pocho cops to visit me. I got your plate number, so I can find you if I got a grudge."

I smiled. "Message received."

Back in my car, I wiped the sweat from my forehead with the sleeve of my jacket and then started the motor. The two young gang members who had stood behind Pedro "Mescal" Herrera now stood in front of my car and stared open-mouthed as I backed out of the parking space and slowly accelerated toward the police department.

Chapter 26

Helen greeted me when I returned from my interview with Herrera's gang. "Get anything good?" she asked.

"Nothing to help the D.A. In fact, the information I found might damage the claims of the victim"

"Same here," Helen said. "Not much from the woman who was the sister of Agosta's friend in Ohio. She and her brother haven't spoken in more than five years, and they weren't on friendly terms while teenagers in high school. But the lunchroom acquaintance is a different story."

I had hoped Helen would uncover something good for the D.A., but she had already prepped me for the opposite. "So, what did you learn?"

"The woman's name is Sandra Ahearn. In high school, her last name was Reilly. She says she sat at the same lunchroom table with Margo Borst for three years in high school. Margo had a sweet tooth, usually getting double desserts and drinking coke at lunch every day."

"So, what does she know about Margo's FF activities?"

"She remembers Margo and the other girl— somebody named Zeena—talking about sex quite often and about FF's several times."

"Really?"

"Yeah. She remembers Zeena would ask Margo

questions about sex, and Margo seemed to know the answers to most of her questions. It was like Margo had a lot of experience and Zeena was filing her comments and information away for future reference."

"What about the FF stuff? Does Mrs. Ahearn know anything specific about it?"

"She remembers Margo suggesting to Zeena that she ought to get an FF. Zeena didn't like the idea, but Margo suggested it several times. She also remembers wondering if Margo had an FF of her own. Back then, it made sense that Margo might, especially since she knew so much about sex."

"Would she be willing to draft a deposition if we need one?"

"She said she would. She's got nothing to hide, and if it will help somebody, she's willing to tell what she remembers."

"Did you tell her the accusation was potentially wrongful to the accused?"

"Nope. Just told her Margo was possibly a rape victim, and we needed information about her character."

"The D.A. isn't gonna be happy about this. Can you write up what you learned and give it to me before the end of the day?"

"It's already in your email as a Word file. I can make you a hard copy if you want."

"You've already saved me at least half a day's work, Helen. I owe you bigtime."

"How about lunch at Ruby's Red Hots next week?"

"You can count on it."

****

Charles Claiborne arrived at his office at nine in

the morning. Sitting on his desk was a ten-page report I had written and addressed to ATTN: District Attorney Claiborne. "Poor bastard probably typed all night," Claiborne muttered.

He asked his secretary to cancel all his morning appointments and to bring him a cup of black coffee, "that Death Wish stuff." When she brought the coffee, he asked her to close his office door so he could read in peace and quiet.

What he read was what he had hoped he would not have to read. The evidence garnered through many interviews, including the depositions of the plaintiff and the defendant, two FBI reports, the County's medical examiner's report, and interviews with a dozen potential witnesses, could be summarized thusly:

Although Mrs. Margo Lumpas has accused West Virginia Judge Michael Agosta of rape while she was in high school, all signs point to her voluntary participation in an "FF" relationship with the accused. The relationship resulted in her becoming pregnant, a fact she told nobody at the time, including the teen father of her child. She gave birth to the child unassisted in an abandoned house. Medical evidence suggests the child was premature and died during or immediately following birth. She buried the child in a shallow grave in the dirt-floor basement of an abandoned house. She was seventeen at the time and confided in nobody. Recommended outcome: The District Attorney's office should drop the case against Judge Agosta and apologize profusely for his unwarranted arrest. The D.A. should consider perjury charges against Mrs. Lumpas for unfounded accusations which led to a false arrest.

Claiborne buzzed his secretary.

"Yes, sir?"

"Call Bart Jones and Helen Martin and instruct them to meet in my office at ten thirty."

"He read my report," I said to Helen when she called to ask if I knew what the meeting was about. "It's not what he was hoping for. He wanted to hang Agosta, to bury his alibi in proof that he was a rapist and child murderer. Instead, I gave him just the opposite."

At ten thirty, Helen and I were waiting nervously in steel and padded vinyl chairs outside the D.A.'s office. We could hear Claiborne speaking loudly on the phone, but we could not discern many words over the tone of anger in his voice. When the phone on his secretary's desk buzzed, I looked at Helen. "Here we go."

"He's ready for you now," the secretary said.

We rose hesitantly from our chairs and walked with trepidation into Claiborne's office. His secretary followed us and closed the door behind her as she exited the office.

"Sit down, you two," Claiborne said, pointing abruptly at the chairs in front of his desk. His tie had been loosened and his collar was unbuttoned. His shirt sleeves were rolled up to his elbows

I did not feel like sitting down. I had been sitting on a chair in my dining room late into the night as I typed the report which I was certain had angered the D.A. But what was I to do? The facts were clear, and the recommendations in my report were probably the best course of action.

"I want to get something out of the way up front,"

Claiborne said. "I'm not angry with you two. If I'm angry at anyone, I'm angry at myself for arresting Judge Agosta and having him extradited to New York before we had completed our investigation. I was hungry for a big kill and thought he was it. Instead, I probably killed myself. I won't be surprised if the County Legislature wants my head on a platter."

"It can't be that bad," I said.

"I was just on the phone with the County Manager. Agosta is already suing the County for false arrest. Do you think he knows something? You didn't tell him what your investigation uncovered, did you?"

"No, sir," I replied. "You know he was running for a seat on the State Court of Appeals in West Virginia. This lawsuit is probably some kind of political ploy."

"Well, the County Manager is pissed about the lawsuit because he sees money flying out of the budget to cover the claim. And the budget's already too tight to squeeze any more blood out of George Washington's eye."

"Doesn't the County carry insurance against lawsuits?"

"Yeah, it's supposed to, but I think the CFO was late in paying the premium during last spring's coronavirus pandemic."

"Oh shit," Helen said.

"I think that's what the County Manager said when the CFO told him about the mistake. Hopefully, the insurance company accepted the late payment, and the County is covered."

"What's the plan of action?" I asked.

"We're all going to meet with Judge Middleton this afternoon to review the case and see what he wants to do with it. Confidentially, there's noise from the governor's office that a second wave of the pandemic is headed this way before the end of November. The virus has mutated into almost a dozen strains, and the CDC hasn't determined which vaccine to recommend as the national preference. If we go to trial, we may be back where we were last spring."

"You mean with jurors sequestered in rooms at the Holiday Inn and watching the proceedings on closed circuit television?" Helen asked.

"Yeah and debating the verdict via Zoom. It was a shitshow last spring and it won't be any better if it happens again."

"What time and where is the meeting?" I asked.

"Judge's chambers, one o'clock. You'd both better be there in case he has any questions."

Chapter 27

Although she had prepared it, Margo Lumpas could not eat her spaghetti dinner. Instead, she just twirled the noodles around her fork with a worried look on her face.

Zoe and Louie finished quickly, both leaving red dots of sauce around their plates on the kitchen table.

"Can we have ice cream sandwiches?" Zoe asked.

Margo didn't respond.

Sitting across the square table from Margo, Henry nodded. "Sure. Why don't you take them up to your playroom."

The kids put their dirty dishes in the kitchen sink, took their desserts from the side freezer of the refrigerator, and hurried upstairs to turn on the television. *The Voice* would be on in fifteen minutes, and they did not want to miss their favorite show.

Henry reached across the table and took Margo's clammy hand in his. "It's probably just a preliminary meeting to establish the protocol for the trial, sweetheart."

Margo pushed her plate of spaghetti away, her eyes betraying her inner fear. "I spoke with Lance about an hour before you got home. He says it's unusual for any judge to call a meeting of both parties before a trial like this, and we're just going to have to see what he has to say and play it by ear."

Henry released his grip on Margo's hand and sat upright. "Our principal called us into a brief meeting after school today," she continued. "The District is anticipating word from the Governor that all students may have to 'shelter in place' again, right after Thanksgiving. He told us that rumors are spreading around the globe that China's pandemic is back. If that happens, I'll be teaching online again, like last spring. Maybe the meeting with Judge Middleton is related to another wave of coronavirus."

"I hope that's all it is."

****

Audrey paced the floor of their hotel room, still in her pink flannel pajamas. Michael sat glumly against the headboard of the queen-sized bed they had shared for the past few weeks, not really noticing that Audrey had walked in front of the television with each pass across the room.

When her phone rang, Audrey stopped her pacing and answered it. It was Jake Lomax.

"Did you hear from Brockbank?" Jake asked.

"Yes," Audrey replied. "He says we have a pre-trial meeting with Judge Middleton at one o'clock. I've tried to get Michael moving, but he's not interested in showering and shaving for this meeting."

"Put him on."

Michael took the cell phone from Audrey with a look of annoyance. "Good morning, Jake."

"Audrey says you're not planning to dress for your meeting with the judge."

"I'm not feeling too motivated. It's uncommon for a judge to pull two warring parties together before a trial. I'm assuming it's bad news...maybe a negotiating tactic…maybe a delay. I can't afford to sit in this damn motel room any longer. I may have to send Audrey out to find a job so we can pay the bill."

"Come on, Mike. You know better than this. How would you regard a defendant who came before you looking and smelling like a Skid Row bum? Do us all a favor and take a shower, shave, and dress in your best suit. When you meet with Judge Middleton, you'll not only be making a statement about yourself, but you'll be making a statement about all West Virginians."

"What do you think he might be up to?"

"The judge? No telling. But you can't show any signs of disrespect."

Michael sighed. "Yeah, you're probably right. What time is it, anyway?"

Audrey looked at the gold watch Michael had given her for her birthday. "It's almost eleven thirty. You've got to get moving. Tell Jake 'Goodbye.'"

"Never mind," Michael told Jake, "Audrey got her watch out quicker than you did."

"Watch? Does anyone wear those these days? I was trying to figure how to move from 'phone' to 'clock' on this damn 'smart phone.'"

"I'll show you how, when and if we get back to West Virginia."

"Fine. I'll take that as a promise and an expectation of service to be rendered. Meanwhile, take a damn shower and shave your ugly face, Mike."

Michael rolled off the bed and walked into the shower, handing Audrey's phone back to her along the way. "I guess I got my marching orders."

"Why didn't you move when *I* asked you to?" Audrey asked.

Edward S. Baker

****

When Michael and Audrey arrived at the courthouse, they parked in a metered space, using a credit card to purchase three hours of time and leaving a receipt of payment on their car's dashboard. Then they climbed the marble steps to the entrance, where they passed through a metal detector and were wanded by a security guard before approaching a reception desk, where they were told to take the elevator to the sixth floor. There, they were directed to waiting room 6A, a room which was twelve feet deep and thirty feet wide. Inside, an armed security guard directed them to oak benches on his right. The Lumpases were already seated to his left.

As they sat, Michael stared past the security desk at Margo, whose eyes were downcast, afraid to look up and meet his. She appeared different than he had envisioned her. Now a middle-aged woman, her dark brown hair had become salt and peppered, and she had put on at least thirty pounds. Michael wondered how he could ever have lain naked with her so many years ago.

When Michael and his wife entered Room 6A, Margo had looked up and upon recognizing Michael had cast her eyes downward so Henry would not see her looking at him. Because her leg was touching Henry's, she felt his muscles tighten at the Agosta's arrival. Margo looked up at Henry, who puffed his chest and glared at Michael's every movement until he sat down on the benches at the far end of the room. Margo knew every fiber of Henry's being wanted to seek some form of revenge against Michael. She feared what Henry might do if provoked.

Time seemed to creep as both couples waited, the

154

tension between them growing. Then the door to Room 6A opened again, and both Lance Freeborn and Lester Brockbank came in together, smiling and chatting with each other. Freeborn turned and waved at the Lumpases as he approached them. Brockbank simply walked to the Agostas and put out his hand to shake with both Michael and Audrey.

"You know the other lawyer?" Henry Lumpas asked Freeborn.

"Yeah, we're in Rotary together. He's a nice man and a good attorney."

"He can't be too nice if he's defending that bastard."

"It's only a job, Henry," Freeborn said. He turned to Margo. "How are you feeling this morning? I have a sense we'll all feel better in an hour."

Margo simply nodded at him and returned her gaze to the floor.

Ten minutes passed and then the door to Room 6A opened again. A police officer announced, "Lumpas and Agosta. Follow me please."

Henry jumped to his feet. Freeborn offered Margo his hand and helped her rise. The Lumpases and their attorney exited the room before the Agostas stood.

"What do you think?" Michael asked Brockbank as he offered Audrey a hand.

"I think we're going to come out of this okay."

"Why makes you say that?" Audrey asked.

"Call it a premonition."

Chapter 28

When they entered the meeting room adjoining Judge Middleton's chambers, both the Agostas and the Lumpases noticed other people seated against the wall. Helen and I were two of them. Both couples knew us because we had interviewed them. The other person, a large man with a grumpy face was an unknown to both couples-- District Attorney, Charles Claiborne.

Judge Middleton entered the room from his office, wearing his official black judicial robe. As he did, both Lance Freeborn and Lester Brockbank started to rise, but the judge motioned for them to sit. "This is an informal hearing, gentlemen," he said.

The judge examined several sheets of paper and then introduced himself, first to the Lumpases and then to the Agostas. As he did, the door to his office opened and his secretary entered carrying a notepad and a tape recorder.

"This is my secretary, Phyllis Reedy. She will transcribe the comments made by all parties in this meeting and send copies to the opposing attorneys in case someone wishes to challenge whatever decision we make here today."

Brockbank and Freeborn both nodded.

"Let's begin, then," the Judge said. "I have before me a copy of the investigating officers' report, with summaries of each interview they conducted. Also included are the sworn statements of the accused and the accuser."

Henry Lumpas squirmed in the sudden discomfort of his chair. The term "accuser" seemed so harsh and belittling, as though names of individuals were of lesser importance than their roles in this case. *Why couldn't the judge simply have said "the statements of Mrs. Lumpas and Mr. Agosta"?*

The judge then summarized the evidence which had brought the case forward—the bones of a deceased baby, Mrs. Lumpas' admission of the baby's birth and questionable death, and her charge of repeated rape by Mr. Agosta when both were teenagers at Willow Falls High School.

The judge noticed Audrey Agosta was fiddling with something in her purse. "What are you doing, Mrs. Agosta?"

"I…uh…I was…uh…"

The judge turned to the District Attorney. "Charlie, would you please take Mrs. Agosta's purse and examine what she's got in there that's so all fired important. It had better not be a handgun."

Claiborne rose from his seat and took Mrs. Agosta's purse. As he did, her left hand slipped out and everyone could see she was holding a small digital tape recorder.

"Dammit, now," the judge said. "You're going to get a written transcript, Mrs. Agosta. Turn that thing off and give your purse to the District Attorney."

Audrey fumbled with the tape recorder and then handed it to Charlie Claiborne. He verified that it had been shut off, plopped it back into her purse, and set her purse on the end of the table, away from Audrey's reach.

"Now," the judge said, "I hope we can move along." He puffed on his glasses, wiped them on the sleeve of his robe, and adjusted them on the bridge of his bulbous nose. He turned to Michael Agosta. "These charges against you are severe. Some say they're worse than murder because the evil and injury inflicted upon rape victims live within them forever. Granted, you were only seventeen at the time, but in this state, you would have been tried as an adult back then, and if found guilty you would still be serving time today."

Michael nodded. He recognized the judge was lecturing not only him, but also Margo. It was a tactic he, himself, had used in several pre-trial meetings. By beginning with the grave situation of the accused, he would next turn to the victim and cast seeds of doubt upon her claim. It was more than Michael could have hoped for. Seated beside him, Lester Brockbank patted Michael's knee under the table and nodded.

Next, the judge read excerpts from witness testimony, beginning with Michael's own statement and followed by a few who knew him back then:

"We were FFs."

"I thought Michael was gay because he wasn't interested in any girls, even the easy ones."

"Michael seemed to grow more confident during his junior year, as though he knew some things about girls that none of the rest of us knew."

Then the judge picked up a sheet of paper and turned to Margo. "You've brought grave charges against a man you haven't seen in twenty years, a man who is highly regarded in his home community. So, what did witnesses who knew you back then say about you?" The judge removed his glasses and cleaned them on his robe again.

"A former student testified whenever she would ask Margo questions about sex, Margo seemed to know the answers to most of her questions."

"I remember one time she talked to me about how I should get an FF. She said it sounded like a good thing."

"Margo said she had been thinking about doing it, herself…becoming an FF…and she said she had a guy she thought might be interested."

The judge stopped there. Margo was sniffling into a tissue.

"I'm sorry for the pain these statements cause either of you, the defendant or the plaintiff," the judge said. "But now I want to read an excerpt from the investigators' report." The judge picked up a stapled document and flipped through the pages until he found the summary and recommendations. "Now this is according to the investigators, who struggled tirelessly to find people who remembered both parties in this case.

"All signs point to Mrs. Lumpas' voluntary participation in an 'FF' relationship with the accused. The relationship resulted in her becoming pregnant, a fact she told nobody, including the teen father of her child. She gave birth to the child unassisted in an abandoned house. Medical evidence suggests the child was premature and died during or immediately following birth. She buried the child in a shallow grave in the dirt-floor basement of the abandoned house. She was seventeen at the time and confided in nobody. Recommended outcome: The District Attorney's office

should drop the case against Judge Agosta…The D.A. should consider perjury charges against Mrs. Lumpas for unfounded accusations which led to a false arrest."

Margo burst into a wail. Henry pounded his fist on the table and then pointed at Michael Agosta and yelled at the judge. "Are you saying my wife voluntarily participated in an FF relationship with this man?"

The judge gave him a stern look. "I'm not saying anything. This is the conclusion of two highly trained investigators who spent countless hours digging through documents and interviewing men and women who knew both parties in this case. Unless your wife can provide otherwise convincing evidence, I am inclined to follow the recommendations of two professional investigators."

Henry turned to his wife. "Margo, you have to give the judge the names of people who can support your claim, or this rapist will get off scot-free."

Margo continued wailing. "It's too long ago," she sobbed. "I never told anybody. I've never been an FF."

"Bullshit," Michael bellowed at the Lumpases.

"Order! Order!" the judge demanded, slamming his hand on the tabletop. "Mrs. Lumpas, I apologize that the County's investigators were not able to substantiate any element of your claims against the defendant. Do you have any further evidence to present to the court to substantiate your accusation of rape?"

Still crying, Margo shook her head.

"In that event, this case cannot proceed to trial. I hereby drop the charges against Michael Agosta. Judge Agosta, you are free to return to your home and life in West Virginia."

Lester Brockbank raised his hand and was

acknowledged by the judge. "Your honor, we request consideration of the court that the plaintiff reimburse the Agostas for the expenses they suffered as the result of these false charges, including lost wages, room and board, travel expenses, and attorney fees."

"Request granted. Please submit a copy of those expenses to the Lumpas' attorney and to the court."

Henry stood and yelled at Judge Middleton. "That's unfair. First, he rapes my wife and then he gets his expenses paid? I won't hear of it."

Lance Freeborn took Henry by the arm. "Quiet down, Henry, or you may face contempt of court for threatening a judge."

"This is bullshit," Henry yelled at the judge.

"Mr. Freeborn, please escort Mr. Lumpas out of this room, or I will have him arrested," the judge demanded.

Freeborn pushed Henry toward the door. "Come on, Henry. It's over. You don't need an arrest on your record. I know you don't like it, but someone is upset after every pre-trial hearing. It just happens to be your turn."

Margo followed Henry and Lance Freeborn into the hallway. Lance asked Margo to wait by a water fountain while he escorted Henry to the men's room to calm him down.

Michael and Audrey Agosta were standing at the end of the hallway chatting with their attorney. After Lester Brockbank shook Michael's hand and entered the elevator, Margo approached the Agostas. As Margo neared, Audrey opened her purse, shuffled a few items around, and retrieved her lipstick and compact. While Michael and Margo talked, Audrey focused on freshening her lipstick

"It's been a long time, Michael," Margo said, her eyes still red and puffy from crying in the meeting room.

"I'm sorry you were pregnant when my family left Willow Falls."

"It's not your fault." Margo stammered for a moment. "Well, I guess we both were at fault. But the baby was a preemie and was born dead."

"So why did you accuse me of rape?"

"Oh God, I'm so sorry to have dragged you through this. My husband is *very* conservative. When they found those bones…I could never tell Henry I was an FF or I would have become cheapened in his eyes. He'd have divorced me on the spot for being unfit to be a mother and his wife. At least now, with this behind us, I think maybe we can move forward with our lives, as if this never happened."

"What about *my* life, Margo? I've lost my judgeship, and my campaign for the West Virginia Supreme Court of Appeals is in shambles because of you and this rape accusation."

"I'm sorry, Michael, truly sorry."

"I'm now unemployed and disgraced in my community."

"I'm sorry. But you don't know Henry. I just couldn't tell him I had ever been an FF because it would have ruined my life."

"What about mine?" Michael ran his fingers through his hair and then pointed a shaking finger at Margo's face. "You're a selfish bitch."

Chapter 29

Michael and Audrey packed their bags, checked out of the Holiday Inn, and set the GPS in Audrey's green Volvo station wagon for the New York State Thruway. They planned to follow the Thruway to Route 88 West, find Route 81, and head south toward West Virginia.

As they drove toward the Crosstown Parkway, Audrey saw Verrigni's Quick Sack and asked Michael if he'd pull over for a cup of coffee for the road. As Michael turned into the parking lot, Audrey noticed a United States Postal Service Branch Office was located next door to the convenience store.

"Michael, you go buy the coffee, and I'll meet you back in the car."

"Cream or half and half?"

"Just like home."

"Half and half, it is."

Inside the Post Office, Audrey held her tiny digital tape recorder to her ear. After a moment she smiled. "This will do just fine."

The postal clerk heard Audrey mumbling to herself. "Can I help you, miss?" He was an older black man, dressed in an official USPO uniform and wearing a sincere smile beneath his short-cropped mustache.

Audrey showed him the small tape recorder. Do you have an envelope that will handle something this size without breaking it?"

"Over on that rack we got lots of padded envelopes. Just pick the one you want, miss."

Audrey opted for the smallest padded envelope. Using the ballpoint pen she found on the customer desk, she addressed the envelope to *Mr. Henry Lumpas, teacher, Marshfield High School, Marshfield, NY.* Then she slipped the tape recorder inside, sealed the envelope, and handed it to the postal clerk.

He plopped the envelope onto his electronic scale. "That will be three dollars and eighty-seven cents."

Audrey smiled and handed the clerk a five-dollar bill. "It's worth every penny."

Chapter 30

As authorities had predicted, a new strain of coronavirus arrived in the United States a few days after Michael and Audrey drove out of New York State. Potential national epicenters were identified as San Francisco, Chicago, Dallas, Miami, and of course, New York City. Fearing rapid spread of the virus, "shelter-in-place" orders were issued from the White House and, as in the recent string of annual pandemics, the practices of social distancing and wearing face masks became the norm. Schools returned to online instruction on alternate days, restaurants served seated guests only in Plexiglas cubicles or socially distanced on outside patios, and emergency hospitals were once again erected in areas of population congestion.

I was at my desk on the morning of November fourth. It was election day, except the second wave of the nasty pandemic had forced the governor to shut down the New York State government for six months. Part of his action included moving the statewide elections to May. Of course, the governor was up for re-election and his opponent was very popular and, according to the polls, was the probable winner if the election were to be held in November.

It was a warm day for November. The local weatherman had predicted highs in the mid-seventies. So, I was wearing khakis and a white short-sleeved shirt, exposing the tattoo of a rooster on my left forearm and a fox on my right. I needed a haircut, but it would have to wait until the weekend, when Rachel would give me a scissors cut after I dyed her hair to hide her graying roots.

The phone on my desk rang. It was the desk sergeant. "There is a guy named Armando who needs to see you on an important matter."

"Send him up," I said. I fumbled in my desk drawer until I found an N-95 face mask, an all-important social distancing requirement before conversing with anyone, especially at my desk.

A heavy-set man wearing green twills and hobnail boots of the labor class entered the room at the far end. He said something to the woman at the first desk and then was directed toward me. As he approached, I raised my hand and waved the man forward.

"Armando Lambrucci," the man said, not offering his hand. He was wearing a hand-made face mask which bore a dozen yellow smiley faces, and he was carrying a large brown paper bag, its top tightly rolled.

"Bart Jones. How can I help you?"

"You the guy who solved the case with the baby's bones?"

"Yeah. We called the little guy 'BabyX.'"

Lambrucci plopped into the steel and vinyl chair across the desk from me. "I'm the guy who dug up the bones with my excavator."

I grinned behind my facemask. "Aha. That's where I know your name. You were interviewed by Helen Martin, who assisted me on the case."

"Yeah."

I waited a moment and then asked again. "So,

what's up? How can I help you?"

Lambrucci twisted awkwardly in his chair. "I got a confession to make."

I waited, then raised my palms upwards and motioned with my fingers for Lambrucci to give me his confession.

Finally, Lambrucci got the message. "There was more than one set of bones."

"Really? Another baby?"

"Wasn't no baby. The second set was a full-grown person. It wasn't in the basement of the house, neither. It was in the detached garage, buried maybe two feet down."

"So why didn't you report it?"

"My boss was P.O.'d about losing two months construction time when you police shut us down because of them baby's bones. He told me to bury the second set in the dirt of my dump truck and to keep my mouth shut or I'd never work again in Willow Falls."

"So, where are the bones now?"

"There's a bunch of dirt on a vacant lot on Clement Street. Got a sign there that asks for donations of clean fill. We been dumping stuff there for over a year. Eventually the low land will have enough fill to spread out and somebody can build a business or something there."

"Does that mean we'll have to dig through a bunch of dirt mounds to try to find the skeleton?"

"Ritchie can probably narrow it down for you. He drives the dump truck. I told him to take special care of that load. He'll probably remember where he dumped it."

I held my hands as though I were praying and

tapped my fingertips together.

"Am I in trouble?" Lambrucci asked.

"Not yet. I'll need you to write a deposition. Then, I'm going to have to chat with your boss. I think I can protect you from getting fired."

Lambrucci opened the paper bag. I brought you some stuff, too. Ain't much, but it'll prove what I'm saying is true."

"Let's see it."

Lambrucci reached in and pulled out a human bone. "This is one of the bones. I dug it out of the bed of the dump truck when the crew was on lunch break."

I thought it looked like a shin bone. I raised my hands in excitement. "Jesus, don't keep handling it. You'll contaminate the DNA."

"I've touched it a lot over the past few months. Didn't know I shouldn't."

I pulled a large clear plastic bag from my bottom desk drawer and put the bone in it. "I'm going to have to send this to the State labs for examination and testing."

Lambrucci reached into the paper bag again. "This too?"

When I looked up, Lambrucci was holding a black leather jacket which still bore signs of having been buried in orange dirt. Four semi-corroded chrome stars were riveted into the leather on each shoulder and a string of similar stars followed the hem at the waistline. All the white thread stitching was stained orange. "This was with the bones."

I borrowed a plastic bag from another detective and carefully plopped the jacket into it. "Another item for State Forensics."

At my direction, Lambrucci was escorted by a junior officer to an interrogation room where he wrote his deposition in pencil on a sheet of lined paper, including Richie's name and telephone number. Somebody from Forensics was going to have to enlist Richie's assistance to find the dirt pile on Clement Street and sift through it for bones and possible additional evidence. Probably a couple of interns and a low-level staffer.

Chapter 31

After boxing the leg bone and leather jacket for shipment to the New York State Forensics Labs, I walked to Helen Martin's office and invited her out to lunch.

Helen's face lit up. "You buying?"

She had been reviewing case files all morning and her eyes showed her fatigue. She was dressed in a brown pants suit I had seen her wear before. Today, though, her jet-black hair was pulled into cornrow braids that looked to me like they might be painful. And her coronavirus facemask was a colorful print, reminiscent of the tropics.

"Sure, if you're not ordering lobster or prime rib."

"Is this a date, handsome? If it is, I'll leave my purse locked in my desk drawer because a nice guy like you wouldn't drop a girl off in the middle of town without a ride home."

"Yeah, do that. I'm not expecting you'll need to pull your piece out at McDonald's."

"Whoa, I thought this was a date. What kind of Don Juan takes a good-looking woman to Mickey-D's? Thought we might be eating hotdogs or maybe fish fry."

"You know a good fish fry place? I only know of the combo Mexican and fish place on the west side. Everything there's too salty for my taste."

"Yeah, I know a good fish fry. It's a little out of the way place called 'Captain Mambo's.' You probably drove past it a few times but didn't think you belonged in there. You were right. But you'll be with me, and the brothers won't give you no grief." Helen pulled back her brown sports jacket, exposing the grip of a .357 magnum in her armpit. "Besides, I always bring an equalizer when I go someplace where the men won't leave a lady to her own business."

We drove across town and into a minority neighborhood. I followed Helen's directions and soon parked on the street in front of a flat-roofed white brick building with a large aluminum ventilator fan spinning on its roof. The words "Capt. Mambo" were scrawled above the door and front window in red paint over a royal blue background. I figured the blue was supposed to represent the ocean. And I thought, perhaps, the red paint signified this establishment was protected or maybe run by the Bloods, another gang of notoriety in Willow Falls.

Helen entered first, and I followed her. All eyes turned to stare at me. There was no question I did not belong. In fact, my presence was probably offensive to some. This was their place, an establishment owned and exclusively intended for people of color. I wished I had not asked Helen out for lunch because McDonalds would have been more welcoming to people of any color. Here, though, my whiteness was an irritant to the clientele.

"Hey. Helen," I whispered, "are you sure about this place? I'd be happy to buy you a prime rib at Garrity's if you'd rather."

Helen laughed. "Now you know how a sister feels

when she's the only woman of color in a restaurant in Whiteyville. Come on, now. Just step up and order something that looks good. I told you you'll be okay 'cause you're here with me."

I ordered a shrimp and fries basket. Helen ordered fried halibut and fries. Both of us got unsweetened iced teas. We found a small rectangular table near the front window and sat down. Two men at the closest table got up and moved when I sat down.

"Don't mind them, Barty. They're just envious 'cause you out with the best-looking sister in this city. They know they ain't got a chance 'cause you got a good job and plenty of money."

"Or they know I'm a cop."

"Or that, too"

I lifted my facemask, put an entire shrimp into my mouth, and pulled off the tailfin. While I was chewing, I started talking, dropping a few crumbs onto the table. "I had an interesting morning. BabyX is back."

Helen flicked a small piece of fried batter off the table and onto the floor. "Do tell?"

"Yeah. Looks like there was another skeleton on the property where BabyX was found. This one was full grown and in the garage. All I have right now is one leg bone and a black leather biker's jacket, but I think I've got a location on the rest of the bones."

"Murder?"

"Too soon to tell. Could be just an overdose or a homeless guy who bought the farm on a cold night. Except he was buried in a shallow grave, so it looks like a murder. You want in? I could use your help."

"If the captain says I can help you, I'll do anything to get away from my desk." Helen wiped grease off her fingers with a brown paper napkin. "If the dead bone turns out to be a guy, he probably got what he deserved, especially in this neighborhood."

"Okay, so you have a thing about men, too. It seems to run in you female detectives." I took a gulp of iced tea. "See what you can work out with the chief when we get back to the station. I've got a three o'clock appointment with Cabrillo Construction and it would be great to have you along. Might lead to an arrest."

****

After lunch, Helen met with the chief and got permission to push a few cases onto the back burner while she helped me wrestle with the new "bone case," beginning with interviewing the owner of Cabrillo Construction. She rode with me through the downtown of Willow Falls and to the north end, where many trucking firms and warehouses cluttered the forgotten streets.

Cabrillo Construction's administrative offices were located on Draper Street at one end of an aged warehouse that housed miscellaneous materials to be used in building construction or renovation. Pickups, dump trucks, backhoes, bulldozers, paving rigs, and cranes were parked in the fenced area alongside the warehouse. Clearly, for a brand-new company they were well-funded, causing me to wonder if they were legitimate or maybe a shill operation supported by the Columbian drug traffickers whose products seemed to be everywhere in Willow Falls. I planned to report my suspicions to the chief later in the day.

I held open the sticker-laden glass door so Helen could walk into the air-conditioned office before I did. I showed my badge to the secretary and told her we had an appointment with Mr. Diego Fernando Cisneros.

"Yes, sir. He's expecting you." She held the receiver to her ear and touched a button on her phone. "Yes, sir." She looked up at us. "He's been waiting for you. He expected you half an hour ago and doesn't have much time before his next appointment."

The secretary escorted us through a swinging door and into an un-air-conditioned area where the loud noises of drills and nail guns pierced the air. Helen covered her ears, but I just took the assault upon my eardrums like punches from an opponent in a boxing ring.

Cisneros' office was over-warm. Its walls were constructed of inexpensive whitewashed paneling anybody could have purchased at an outlet store for less than five dollars per sheet. Shelves on the walls were unpainted pine boards which rested on white triangular metal supports. The floors were bare concrete, but they had been waxed.

Cisneros rose when we walked in. He was a large man of Hispanic extraction, with long black hair, slicked backwards on the top and sides. His facial pores looked like they belonged on a golf ball. A suit coat was hanging on a hook near his desk, and when he greeted us, he was wearing a striped short-sleeved shirt accented by black suspenders. His forearms were muscular, and he wore a ring on his right pinkie that I had seen before in crime seminars. It was the insignia of the Los Equis Cartel. The same symbol was centered on the black facemask that covered his mouth, but not his nose.

I shook his hand, noting that it was hot and sweaty, and then introduced Helen as my "colleague."

"Sorry about the heat in this office. I keep it warm to remind me of my home in Mexico," Cisneros said. "How can I help you?"

"We've come for information about the other skeleton found on the Spencer Street property," I said.

"Other skeleton?"

"Yup, the large skeleton your company unearthed in the detached garage out back. Why didn't you immediately notify us of the discovery?"

"You got no proof of any skeleton other than that kid's."

"That's where you're wrong. We have a leg bone and a jacket the skeleton was wearing at the time your men dug it up. And a deposition from someone who was there when it was discovered."

"Who told you guys that? Whoever he is, he's a liar. My men never dug up a second skeleton."

Helen pointed her finger in my direction. "He told you we know about the skeleton. We have part of it and are sifting dirt to find the rest of it. When we do, you'll be arrested for disturbing a crime scene and interfering with a murder investigation."

"Okay, okay," Cisneros said. "So, maybe another one did turn up. It wasn't like the other. It was in a shallow grave. Might just have been buried under a pile of leaves and rubbish until we discovered it when we were tearing down the old garage. Juan stepped on it and his foot went into a soft spot, like a hole. When he pulled his foot out, some ribs or something came up on his boot. Scared him loco."

"Back to my first question," I said. "Why didn't you call the police and report it?"

"Look, the way the skeleton was just lying there in

a pile of leaves, I figured he was just some homeless nobody who bought the farm a few winters ago. Besides, when you guys found the baby's bones, you shut down my project for two months. I couldn't afford another shutdown like that. I've got too much invested, and every day my men don't work is more money lost."

"You got any suspicions the skeleton might have been some kind of gang murder?"

"Why would you ask that? How would I know?"

I smiled and pointed at his pinkie. "That ring you're wearing is a Los Equis symbol."

"Never heard of them. I bought this ring at a pawn shop in Delray Beach."

"Do you have a receipt for that purchase? You might want to get your money back. Some local gangbanger sees it, he might shoot you or slit your throat so he can take your finger with that ring on it back to his leader and get a reward."

Cisneros feigned surprise. "You really think so? Then I guess I'd better look for the receipt. Meanwhile, I'll be sure to take the ring off whenever I'm walking near the street corners downtown."

"You ought to stay in town for the next few days in case the District Attorney issues a warrant for your arrest," Helen said.

"What would he do that for?"

"For withholding evidence of a possible murder, accessory to a murder, and maybe gang-related activity."

Cisneros quickly became serious. "He ought not do that. I have friends."

Helen and I stood and opened the door to leave. I turned to Cisneros. "We'll tell him you said so."

Chapter 32

Michael and Audrey arrived at their home in the suburbs of Charleston, West Virginia, with no fanfare. His acquittal in New York had made only last page news in the local section of the Charleston Gazette. So, before entering Charleston he filled his gas tank a few miles outside of town and then drove directly into his garage without stopping to say hello to neighbors.

News of the resurgent pandemic arrived when the governor shut down the state while they were on the road. The next morning's paper and television newscasts outlined the story of the virus's return, blaming inappropriate social distancing and citizen misuse of face masks as the cause. All West Virginia governmental offices were shut down for at least two weeks and staff was furloughed until the extent of the problem could be assessed by medical professionals.

Most important, however, was due to the pandemic's return, state elections were postponed for six months and were tentatively re-rescheduled for the first Tuesday in May. All elected officials in contested positions would remain in those positions until the various outcomes of the May elections could be determined.

Michael's phone rang a few minutes after noon. "Mikey, are you free to talk?" It was Carl Murphy, one of the men who had encouraged him to run for the State

Board of Appeals.

"Hi, Carl. Yeah, I guess so."

"Just a minute." There was a click on the phone. "I put you on speakerphone so Ben can be part of this conversation."

"Hi, Michael," Ben said. "It's great to know you're back in West Virginia. Good news about the outcome of your legal case."

Michael sat down in his brown leather easy chair. "Thanks, Ben. I wasn't really worried. Well, not too much. It ended up the way I had hoped, except I've lost my position here in Charleston. I expected to be suspended, but not to be fired. I'm going to set a meeting with the County Manager for next week, after I recover from my road trip. I plan to ask to be reinstated."

"Didn't you read the paper this morning, Mikey?" Carl asked. "The County Manager is all over it."

Michael had not yet walked onto his dew-soaked lawn to retrieve it. "Haven't seen it."

Carl sounded excited. "Three different citizens' watch groups have sued that S.O.B. for putting Cynthia into your position. They say it's absolutely nepotism and probably corruption for him to put his wife into your judgeship." Before Michael could say anything, Carl kept going. "But there's more…somebody did some rooting around and they've got the goods on him. Seems he got himself a piece of land and he sold it to the County for five times its value, so they can build a new jail out there. Then, seems he's got partial interest in the construction company that won the contract to build the jail. Maybe he's going to jail, especially since he set his wife up in the position to declare whether or not there's any improprieties in the deal. How could he be so stupid?"

Carl and Ben both started laughing.

****

Four days later, the County Legislature scheduled its regular monthly meeting as an on-line meeting, the County Manager, the Mayor, and the Comptroller broadcasting from the regular meeting room and the legislators attending virtually. As the meeting began, the doors to the meeting room burst open and two dozen members of the Charleston Citizens' Watch group marched into the room chanting and carrying signs which read "Crooks Must Resign" and "Justice for the People." All wore Covid face masks with hideous fangs, reptilian scales, and skeletal teeth on them. Large men pulled the County officials and the mayor from their chairs and took turns shouting at the virtually present legislators, accusing both the County Manager and his wife of corruption and demanding their removal. The protestors held paperwork up to the cameras for the legislators to see.

The next morning, Michael was reading about the hijacking of the meeting when the County Attorney, Nelson Reedy called. "We got a problem, Mr. Agosta. Details of the County Manager's crooked dealings have emerged, thanks to that group last night, and we have asked the Deputy Manager to step into the role of Manager, while charges of corruption are being drafted. Clearly, the County Manager's wife cannot serve as adjudicator of the case, so we are hoping you'd be willing to accept reinstatement as County Court Appellate Judge."

"And what will happen to his wife?"

"She can't testify against him, but we have documents which prove he's been raking in hundreds of thousands of dollars in profits from County coffers. She's complicit in the fraudulent activity. She's going to be released from her position by the County Legislature as of five this afternoon. To put it bluntly, we need you, not only because we need a judge, but because we need one with a record of honesty. One the citizens trust."

"In spite of my recent arrest on rape charges?"

"Especially because of that. You were exonerated."

"I wouldn't mind being back on the bench. Count me in. I'll start work on Monday."

Chapter 33

Margo had not seen or spoken to her sister Darla in more than ten years. Darla had taken a bumpier road in life, rejecting everything her fundamentalist parents stood for and paying the price in her senior year of high school when she came home pregnant. Her parents disowned her, threw her out of the house, and refused her pleas for help when she had difficulty juggling the demands of teen parenthood and low-wage jobs. The best gig of her life was Walmart, but it paid only minimum wage, and she was not able to land that job until her children were in middle school. Until then, she worked a string of chambermaid jobs at local motels where patrons often left before dawn and never put a dollar bill on the pillow for the hired help. She was always some gangbanger's punch and never married the fathers of her two children, though she was only certain of the paternity of her eldest. The father of the youngest could have been any one of half a dozen men.

So, it was a surprise when Margo opened her front door at the sound of the chimes and saw Darla standing there, looking like she was in her mid-fifties rather than her mid-forties. Her face bore deep lines and pock marks, her hair was salt and peppered, her clothes were thrift shop specials, and her flip flops were dirty, with duct tape holding the toe strap together on her left foot.

Margo looked in her driveway and saw Darla had

arrived in a rusted maroon Hyundai with a homemade black air scoop and balled fringe taped to the top of the front windshield. A gold plastic crown was perched above the back seat and centered in the rear window.

Darla snapped her gum. "Well, aren't you gonna ask me in?" she asked, her left hand raised against the door jamb.

"You have anybody with you?"

"Nope. It's your lucky day."

Margo stepped back from the door and let Darla into her foyer. "It's been a long time, Darla. Why now?"

"I just wanted to see you. I read about you in the papers. Even caught a couple of news broadcasts on television, Channel Six, I think. You sure were into some pig slobber, weren't you?"

"Is that why you're here…to gloat?"

"No, I'm here to try to offer you some support, Li'l Sis. I know Mom and Dad would have disowned you, too, if they were still alive. At least I was a senior before I got knocked-up. I thought maybe you'd like to commiserate. You know, tell your older sis all about your woes."

"There's nothing to tell, Darla. The papers got it all. How I was pregnant and delivered the stillborn baby myself. How I buried it. How the construction company found the skeleton. And how DNA ratted me out and ruined my life."

Darla looked into the living room. "Don't look like your life is too ruined. You got a nice place here with decent furniture. You even got some grass out front to mow. I'll bet your refrigerator is full of good things to eat and your babies never went hungry." Darla nodded as she looked around her. "Yup, I'd trade places with you anytime."

Unsure what to do with the sudden appearance of her estranged sister, Margo offered her something to eat or drink.

"Got any beer?"

Margo handed her one of Henry's favorite brown ales.

"Ain't you got something normal…a Bud or a Blue?"

"This is my husband's beer. I drink wine. Would you prefer a glass of chardonnay?"

"Ain't you fancy, now, Missy," Darla cooed. "In my place we only drink Bud or red wine. I get the cheapest I can get by the gallon. If I brought home white wine, I'd get yelled at." Darla looked at the bottle of brown ale as she spun it around in her fingers. "I guess I'll try this stuff. Is it a twist off?"

Margo handed her a church key. "So why are you here, Darla? You haven't given dog poop about me for more than ten years and then here you are out of the blue."

Darla opened the bottle and took a small sip of the brown ale. She was not sure she liked its strange back taste enough to finish the entire bottle. "I got no hidden agenda, Margo, if that's what you're worried about. Except, maybe, when they tore down the house where they found your baby's bones, did they find anything else?"

"Like what?"

"Nothing in particular. Some of the gangbangers I used to date would use that house to shoot up smack. They knew you was using it, too, with that white boy…the one that knocked you up. But they didn't bother you and him none because you were my little sister. That was at least something good I did for you."

"Are you thinking maybe the cops found drugs there?"

"Yeah… or maybe something else. I'm not sure what, but you never know. Maybe a gun would show up or a machete that was used to off somebody. You never know."

"You're scaring me, Darla. All I know is they found my baby's bones. They traced them to me and Michael, and the rest is what you read in the paper. If you're worried about something else that was hidden on the property, I don't know what it is, I don't want to know what it is, and I think you're probably home free."

Darla poured the half-empty bottle of ale into the sink and gave Margo her contact information—a cell phone number, but no address. She also made Margo promise to call her if anything else about the property should come up.

"Gotta go now, Sis," Darla said, smiling. "I been here too long. I been to Marshfield a couple of times, but I'm like some kind of cop magnet. They see my car on these streets, it's for sure they'll stop me, give me the third degree about my business here, and escort me back to the city like I'm some kind of pollution or something."

When Margo closed the door behind Darla, she locked both the knob and the dead bolt. Then crumpled to the floor and wept.

Chapter 34

After the captain's daily briefing, Helen and I drove to the vacant lot on Clement Street to see what progress had been made by the Forensics team. When I brought my sedan to a stop in front of a sign which read CLEAN FILL WANTED, a woman looked up from a table beside a large dirt pile and flipped me the finger.

"Looks like Francine's got a message for you," Helen said.

I smiled and nodded.

We got out of the car and walked across the lot to the largest pile of dirt. The lot sat between a couple of two-family houses in an old middle-class neighborhood. Back in the fifties, this was a side of Willow Falls where it had been good to grow up. All the families watched out for the neighborhood kids, and almost every mother was always home. Those days of innocence were long gone.

Francine Roberts was raking her gloved hands through dirt and small rocks on the sifting table. It was constructed of two by fours and screen wire. A red railroad bandana was draped around her neck. She wore light tan construction boots with thick soles, blue jeans, and a tan broadcloth shirt. "I got a bone to pick with you, Jones," she said.

"Stop with the puns, already," Helen said. "What have you found so far, Frannie?"

"First thing I found was a den of garter snakes living in a couple of cinder blocks at the base of that dirt pile. Scared the bejeesus out of me when they came out in all directions. Thought I got bit, but it was just a scratch from the edge of one of the cinder blocks."

"But nobody got hurt?" Helen asked.

"No, no victims from the attack." She thought for a moment and smiled. "That kid Ritchie, the one who pointed us at this particular pile, grabbed a couple of those snakes by the tails and threw them across the lot. Whipped them around over his head and sent them flying. Strange kid. He laughed the whole time, like he wasn't afraid of them."

"What have you found in your sifting?" I asked.

"Besides a couple of ant hills?"

"Yeah."

Francine pointed at a cardboard box on the ground near the sifting table. "Check those out."

I bent down and picked up the cardboard box, rattling eight oblong white objects, each about an inch long. "Little bones. Toes, maybe?"

"Fingers, I think. The ME will know for sure. But they sure look human to me."

"Bingo," a guy at the top of the dirt pile shouted.

"Whatcha got, Jeremy?" Francine shouted up to him.

"Got a skull. No jaw yet, but it looks intact."

Francine dropped her handful of dirt. "Come on, Jonesy, let's go see what Jeremy has."

We followed Francine around the dirt pile and waited as Jeremy finished climbing down from the top, eight feet above. He was carrying the skull in one hand like a bowling ball, his ring and middle fingers inserted into the eye sockets. "Here it is, boss."

"Excellent." Francine held out two hands and gently pulled the skull off Jeremy's fingers. "You know, Jones, I thought this was going to be a complete waste of time, but it looks like we're gonna find what you've been looking for." She turned to Jeremy. "This was a good find. Go see if you can locate the jawbone or some ribs. I'll send the others around to help you. Three sets of hands are always better than one."

Jeremy climbed back to the top of the dirt pile and slowly pulled dirt away, sifting it through his hands and letting clean dirt tumble toward the bottom of the pile. Francine walked around the pile and said something to two other workers, then returned to Helen and me. "We'll get it all, if it's all here, Jonesy. I'll call you tonight or tomorrow morning with an update."

"Sounds good. Chief's gonna like this," I replied.

****

At eleven the next morning Francine Roberts called to tell me her team had located everything but a pinkie finger and a leg bone. All the bones had been delivered to the medical examiner for processing. I thanked her and then, as I hung up the receiver, I took a handful of morning mail from the clerk who was delivering it on her regular rounds.

The mail included what I had been hoping for, the State Lab's DNA analysis of the one bone and the jacket I had been given by Armando Lambrucci. According to the report, the bone had been a femur belonging to a Hispanic male estimated to have been in his late thirties at the time of death. Based on decomposition, the probable date of death was three years ago, but no more than four. The jacket offered

DNA from multiple sources, most of it corrupted by misuse and moisture damage. However, the lab techs had been able to decipher one of the two words written in indelible ink on the flap of an interior pocket: "Margo." The second word was indecipherable.

"Gotcha," I said aloud.

I walked to Helen's office and asked her to accompany me to the morgue. Together, we took the elevator to the basement. Helen seemed happier than normal, like she knew a secret nobody else did and she was bursting to tell someone. She hummed a tune I did not recognize as the elevator descended.

"Win the lottery last night?" I asked.

"Why you asking me that?"

"Well, you're wearing a bright flowery print dress, your makeup is positive, and you're humming like you found a thousand dollars in your purse."

"Went on a date last night."

"Somebody in the department?"

"Nobody in the department is interested, no matter what I wear or how I act. I s'pose they think you and I got something going on."

I rolled my eyes. "So, who is this new Romeo?"

"A guy that works in Albany. He's some kind of assistant with the Assembly. Does budget development and analysis."

"What's his name?"

Helen raised one eyebrow and smiled. "No way I'm telling you. You gonna call him and give him the third degree and he won't ask me out again. I got to protect my interests."

I looked down at my medium brown wingtips. A line of dirt hugged the sides of the leather, probably left over from my visit to the lot on Clement Street. "You have a pretty low opinion of me."

"I been hanging around with you long enough to know how you do business."

The door to the elevator opened, and Helen scooted out before I could say anything else. She walked ahead of me, her flowery perfume filling the air behind her.

When we entered the morgue, the medical examiner was standing on his plywood platform beside a skeleton, which lay pieced together on a stainless-steel table in the center of the room. He was speaking into a microphone as he examined the body, in much the same manner as a surgeon recites his every move into a recording device during surgery. In a surgeon's case, it is done mostly to protect him from frivolous lawsuits. In the medical examiner's case, it is because the body will be incinerated or buried, so he creates a permanent record in case of unanticipated criminal prosecutions requiring a body.

"What can you tell us about the deceased?" I asked.

Dr. Foster looked at us from above his peach-colored lenses. "No evidence of stabbing or shooting, and no evidence of trauma to the skull. Missing the last two digits on the little finger, right hand. Scratches on the first digit indicate both digits may have been removed by a sharp implement, possibly a knife, but maybe a lawnmower blade or a meat slicer. Forensics said they found the bones in a pile of dirt from a garage. Shallow grave. Could have been an overdose. Could have frozen to death if it happened during winter. Except he was buried, which means somebody found and interred the body."

"You're not giving us any information we haven't already figured out."

"You want more? Next time bring me a fresh cadaver that arrives in one piece, and I'll give you more than you need. You want a DNA workup?"

"Already got it. I had the femur in my hand before I got the location of the skeleton. This guy was Hispanic, late thirties."

"Yeah, that's pretty consistent with what I found. Don't think it was a gang-related murder unless they injected him with something…and that would be abnormal for a gang."

"Yeah, it would. State Lab still has the femur if you want it."

"I don't give a rat's ass about the femur, unless the State Lab gave you a name."

"We're working on a name. State Lab didn't mention one."

Chapter 35

I picked up the phone and dialed the number of the Marshfield Police Department. When the desk sergeant answered, I asked to speak to Chief Parillo.

"Just a minute." The sound of canned music filled my ear, then a loud crackle.

"Parillo here."

"Chief, this is Bart Jones from Willow Falls. I need to set up another interview with Margo Lumpas."

There was a pause with heavy breathing on the other end of the phone, as though Chief Parillo had just run a mile in three minutes. "Listen, Jones, are you harassing one of my citizens? Every time you call me, it's always to question the same poor woman. Her life is already destroyed. You planning on ripping her apart?"

"I got another skeleton. Same location. Got some clothing buried with the skeleton, too. Her name is on it."

The chief snorted into the phone. "All right, I'll call you when I got it set up."

"No need for your part-time policewoman. I'll bring my own."

"Yeah, you do that."

****

The Marshfield PD desk sergeant called me a day later to tell me the interview with Margo Lumpas had

191

been set up for Thursday at eleven in the morning. Her husband also would be in attendance, as would her attorney, Lance Freeborn. I called Helen and had her clear her calendar for that morning.

After all arrangements had been made, I went to lunch at Ruby's Red Hots and then returned to my desk, my breath reeking of onions and hot sauce. Waiting for me was a box from the State Lab, containing both the femur and the leather jacket. I slid the femur into an interoffice envelope and addressed it in care of the Medical Examiner. I laid the jacket on my desk, where it sat for two days.

On Thursday, I rode with Helen to the Marshfield PD because my city-owned sedan was getting an oil change at the city-run garage. Helen had made me put the black leather jacket in a brown paper bag so the red dirt which still clung to it would not drop off inside her car. "Don't want that dead guy's dried stuff all over my nice carpet," she said. "You riding in a car with class." It was a red Toyota Prius with spinning hub caps that belonged on a muscle car, not a suburban grocery hauler. Her floor mats were black after-market specials, and a hibiscus flower aroma disk dangled from her rearview mirror.

We were directed to the interview room by the desk sergeant. "We know where it is," I said.

"The others are already in the room," the desk sergeant replied.

I nodded.

Helen followed me down the short hallway and to the interrogation room. I knocked twice on the door and then held it open so Helen could enter first. Margo and Henry Lumpas and Lance Freeborn were all seated on one side of the small gray metal table. Freeborn was the only one in formal attire. Henry and Margo both wore maroon and gold running suits with the Marshfield Tigers logo.

I reacquainted the Lumpases with Helen and then reached across the table to shake hands with Henry and Lance Freeborn. Lance shook my hand, but Henry Lumpas declined the cordiality.

I opened my notebook and started my digital tape recorder. "I'm sure you're all wondering why I've asked to speak with Mrs. Lumpas again. Actually, I'm investigating a different case, though it seems to intersect with the past one which involved Mrs. Lumpas."

Henry Lumpas leaned forward. "I'm incensed that you won't leave my poor wife alone. Isn't it enough she was humiliated in the local papers by your last investigation? Her so-called friends never call her to play cards anymore. Her social life is in the shitter."

Lance Freeborn reached out and touched Henry gently on his forearm. Henry sat back.

"I'm sorry for the humiliation brought down on your family, Mr. Lumpas, but it wasn't my doing. I was only trying to get to the bottom of a possible murder. What we discovered surprised us all."

Helen gestured toward Margo. "Mrs. Lumpas, I hope things have been well with you since the mistrial."

Before Margo could speak, Henry leaned forward again, almost growling. "She's been paying her dues to society by giving presentations to youth groups and school assemblies about the perils of premarital sex. She relives the shame of her past every time she gives a presentation. But that isn't enough for you, is it,

Detective?"

Lance Freeborn grasped Henry's forearm and pulled him back into his seat.

I lifted the brown paper bag and plopped its contents onto the table. "Let's get to the point of today's interview, shall we?"

Margo's eyes opened wide. "I had a jacket like that when I was a kid."

I folded back the front panel and lifted the flap on the interior pocket, exposing the old writing. "Can you read what it says, Mrs. Lumpas?"

"Yes. It says, 'Margo.' That *is* my old jacket. Where did you find it?"

Lance Freeborn corrected Margo. "My client indicates the jacket is of a similar variety to a jacket she owned as a teenager. She does not claim the jacket is hers, but it bears a striking resemblance to one she owned back then."

"Tell me about your jacket, Mrs. Lumpas," I asked. "How long did you own it. What did you eventually do with it?"

Margo looked at Freeborn and nodded. "I owned a jacket similar to that one when I was a teenager. I used to wear it to school and to sporting events. One day it just disappeared. I asked my parents and my sister if anyone had seen it, but it had just vanished. I never saw it again."

"Sure," I said, smirking.

"Watch your insinuations, bucko," Henry said gruffly.

I wiped the smile off my face and motioned for Helen to continue the questioning.

"This jacket was found with a second skeleton

which was dug up on the same property as your son's skeleton, Mrs. Lumpas," Helen said. "It wasn't found in the basement of the former property, but in a shallow grave in the garage area. The skeleton belonged to a man in his late thirties."

Now Margo understood why Darla had come to visit a week ago. Darla was aware of the possibility a second skeleton would be unearthed. She was also aware of whose skeleton it was and why it was buried there. But Margo wasn't going to throw Darla under the bus. At least not yet.

I saw the change in Margo's expression and the widening of her irises. "Do these details ring any bells for you, Mrs. Lumpas? Do you know the identity of the man who was buried in the garage? Can you tell us how he died? Did you have anything to do with it?"

"No. No. No. No. The existence of a second skeleton on the property is news to me. I personally know nothing about it. I wasn't involved in the murder."

"Murder?" I asked. "We didn't say anything about a murder. Was the victim murdered?"

"I mean, if the person *was* murdered."

Lance Freeborn slapped his hand sharply on the table. "I'm stopping this inquisition here and now, Detective Jones. My client told you she was not aware of the skeleton or the person it was in, and she doesn't know how the man died. Since you have no other relevant questions, we're out of here."

"I have one more question, Mr. Freeborn." I looked directly into Margo's eyes. "Do you know anyone who might have the answers to my questions, Mrs. Lumpas? Anyone?"

Margo's eyes flicked away from me and then returned. She stared angrily into my eyes.

Henry stood and tugged on his wife's arm. "Come on, honey. It's time to go."

Margo stood planted beside Henry and continued to stare at me. Henry tugged on her arm again, and they quietly left the interrogation room together.

Helen held her fist against her lips. "She knows who did it or she knows somebody who knows who did it. The problem's gonna be getting her to sing."

I nodded. "She knows a fish never gets into trouble until it opens its mouth."

Chapter 36

The following Monday Helen came to my desk. She was wearing blue jeans and a green sweatshirt, and the expression on her face told me she was all business. "Maybe we caught a break in the case."

I was writing in my case log. I looked up and dropped my pencil. "How's that?"

"You know that guy who goes by the name 'Mescal'?"

I nodded and picked up my coffee mug.

"Got arrested last night in a brawl on the street in an Italian neighborhood. Something about not paying up on a bet when the Patriots lost a game."

"He's probably already out."

Helen shook her head. "Not yet. He was carrying a piece. Nine-millimeter. Numbers were filed off. Said he found it on the street. D.A.'s holding him for consideration of formal charges."

I chugged the remainder of my coffee and stood. "Let's go see him."

We took the elevator to the basement, passed through the metal detector, and were let into the holding cell area by two armed police officers in uniform. Pedro Herrera was in Cell Four, sitting on the edge of his metal bunk with his elbows on his knees and his chin in his hands.

"Mr. Herrera?" I said.

Mescal looked up. "Oh, it's you. Thought I tol' you not to bother me no more."

"I need your help on another case."

Mescal looked down and shook his head slowly. "I ain't in the frame of mind to help you, gringo. Been all night in this pinta."

"Maybe I can help you if you help me. Maybe get the charges reduced or dropped."

"You askin' me to give somebody up?"

"I don't think so. I just need help in finding my way to the right door."

Mescal thought for a moment. He had been arrested twice before on illegal gun charges. This third arrest might send him up for hard time. He stood and swaggered to the cell door. "What problem you tryin' to solve tha' needs my superior capabilities?"

"Found another skeleton on the lot on Spencer Street. This one buried shallow, like it was done quickly. Found a black leather jacket buried with it. Thought you might know who the dead guy was."

"Don't know the guy. Maybe the jacket."

"We think it belonged to the girl you called 'L'il Margo' when I spoke with you last time"

"It have little silver stars on the shoulders and the bottom, all around?"

"Yup," Helen said.

Mescal looked at Helen as though she was not supposed to be listening in on the conversation, much less making comments or asking questions. His eyes turned back to me. "You know that girl 'Puta-Dee'? She had one like that. Let whoever was doing her wear it, like the jacket was her brand that say, 'this hombre belong to me.' But she didn't own nobody. She was everybody's punch, only she didn't know it."

"Darla Borst? Is she the one you call 'Puta-Dee'?"

"Yeah, I thin' that was her name. Borsk or Borsh or somethin' like that. She had a jacket just like that."

"Did you ever wear her jacket?"

"No, I did her for a while then passed her down to Juaquin. Juaquin wore that jacket a little bit. But he passed her down to L'il Pedro and the jacket went with her. L'il Pedro passed her and the jacket down to Joe Tijuana, who passed her down to Big Pedro, and maybe a couple of others like a hand-me-down blow up doll. Then she jus' disappeared. Quit coming around no more. Haven't seen that puta in years."

"You could use a lesson or two in respect for women," Helen said angrily.

Mescal looked at her and then back at me. He tilted his head in Helen's direction. "She your punch, man? She gotta learn her place."

Helen slammed her palms into the cell door, making it clang loudly. One of the armed men in uniform looked down the corridor. "You two okay?"

I nodded, then turned back to Mescal. "You got any more information? Think you might now remember who the dead guy is?"

"No, I jus' remember that jacket. You go see Puta-Dee. She'll give it up to you. Maybe do something nice for you if you put a bag over her head." Mescal laughed.

"Thanks," I said.

"Hey, Mister Detective, don't forget to get those charges dropped."

Helen and I left the holding cells and rode the elevator back to our second and third floor offices.

"For a gangbanger, he's a real misogynist," Helen hissed. "You aren't gonna help that pig evade those charges, are you?"

"Yeah, I am. Never know when he might come in handy."

Chapter 37

I was outside the prisoner-release door when Pedro Herrera came out of the Willow Falls police department. As Pedro neared, I asked, "Hey, Mescal, you gonna give me the help I need?"

Herrera broke into a big smile and spun in a circle. "I got friends. See how they got me out. All the charges were dropped. Why would I help you?"

"'Cause I'm the only friend you got. Who do you think got your cell unlocked?"

"I helped you yesterday, so we square."

I held up a sandwich bag full of powdered sugar. "Yeah, until I find this bag of coke in your trunk."

Herrera slumped his shoulders. "Aw, don't be doin' that to me, man. Don't be plantin' no bogus stash in my car." He threw his hands up in the air and then flopped them to his side in frustration. "Wha' you wan' now?"

"I want to talk with every man in your club who ever wore Puta-Dee's jacket."

"None of my guys offed that hombre, if that's what you're after. I can promise you that."

I could see Mescal was going to cooperate, so I put the bag of sugar back in my coat pocket. "But maybe one of them knows something that will help me figure out who the dead guy is. That's all I want."

"Nobody gets arrested or nothin'?"

"Nobody gets arrested. I promise."

"Okay. Meet me in Central Park at ten tomorrow morning. I'll have the guys there, and you can talk with them one by one." Pedro looked down at the toe of his boot on the concrete sidewalk. "All except Juaquin. He died a few years back in Troy…but you already know that."

"Yeah. See you tomorrow at ten in Central Park. Maybe by the fishpond? Nice parking there for motorcycles."

"Yeah, tha's good."

****

The morning was spectacular. The sky was Carolina blue with only a few puffy white clouds hovering above the park. The air was warm and promised a hot afternoon, but a cool breeze prevented anybody from perspiring.

I took Helen along for the meeting with the Mexicans, but she stayed in the car, basically to call for backup if I got into trouble. She did not want to stand face-to-face with any chauvinists, anyway. She also filmed the meeting, so the police department would have pictures of the men in question. We would tie names to the faces later. Several bumblebees buzzed her car window, and two hummingbirds jumped between a dozen red tulips which had been planted by city parks personnel.

Pedro "Mescal" Herrera and three of his club members had ridden their Harleys to the fishpond in Central Park and had backed them into parking spaces. I assumed it was in case they needed to exit in haste. The bikes were all black and had wide tires. Three had windshields, but one sported a fairing. Each bike was embellished with specialties of pride. One had a death's head distributor cover, another wore red fringe taped across the top of its windshield, and yet another had a machete scabbard welded to its side frame. The machete, itself, appeared to be easy to remove any time it was needed.

Dressed in black jeans and a brown leather jacket, I spoke briefly with Mescal and then interviewed each man one-on-one out of earshot of the others. I asked each guy the same questions: Did you ever bang the woman called Puta-Dee? Did she give you a jacket? What did it look like? Do you still have the jacket? If not, what happened to it? When you and Puta-Dee broke up, who did she hang around with next? Did you ever see the next guy wear Puta-Dee's jacket? Who did she hang with after she left your club? Do you know the name of the guy who turned up as a skeleton in the garage on Spencer Street? Have you heard anything in the club or on the street about what happened to the guy who was buried in the garage?

When I had finished interviewing each of the three men, I bid farewell to Mescal and wished him happy riding.

Back in the car, Helen was anxious for any information I had acquired.

"It's like this," I said. "They all remember the leather jacket because it was over-sized and anyone could wear it. The jacket went along with Darla to whomever she was sleeping with at the time. It was like a trophy. But nobody knows what happened to Darla. She was hot and heavy with a guy named Miguel...even had a baby with him... but he died in a motorcycle accident on the Thruway three years ago.

She disappeared after the baby was born. Two of the guys asked me, 'Is that puta still alive?' Last thing any of them remembers about her is she was doing smack with some local punks—probably the Clan. One guy assumed that she must have bought the big one by now."

"What about the bones in the garage?"

Only one guy had a clue. He says his sister was involved with something that went down in the garage, but it was four or five years ago, and she didn't want to talk about it back then."

"Did you get her contact information?"

"I got a name and a street. Yellow house with red shutters."

"Then maybe we got something, Jonesy."

"I'm still unsure about Margo. I keep thinking maybe she's involved in this some way."

Helen put her video camera on the console between us. "Well, I think now we know Margo was telling the truth about her jacket. It seems like Darla stole it and wore it to impress or fit in with the Mexicans, at least until she started going steady with one of the gang members. Then, when she settled in with a guy for a while, she gave him the jacket to wear. We gotta assume that whoever the dead guy in the garage was, he probably was Darla's boyfriend."

"Yeah. You think she offed him?"

"Hard to say."

Chapter 38

Judge Michael Agosta had just completed three hours of listening to two attorneys argue against the County's authority to designate a tract of wetlands as "unsuitable for construction." Their hope was to overrule the County's designation on a three-hundred-acre parcel of lowland where they planned to build a private golf course and swim club by filling the wetlands with clean rubble and topping the rubble with three feet of high grade topsoil. The hearing would continue for another week, all accomplished by closed circuit television, in compliance with COVID regulations issued by the governor.

When his phone rang, Michael shut down the closed-circuit television and picked up the receiver. His secretary told him Harold Pollack, head of the West Virginia Republican Party was on the line.

"Put him through," Michael said.

"Go ahead, Mr. Pollack," his secretary said. The phone beeped when she hung up her receiver.

"Judge Agosta? Harry Pollack here."

"Yes, my secretary told me you were on the line. How can I help you, Mr. Pollack?"

"Maybe the question should be 'How can we help each other?' I need to see you in private. Can you come by my hotel room at the Sheraton Four Points tonight, say eight thirty?"

"Nope. It would look clandestine. Why don't you come by my house at eight? My attorney will be at our home for dinner this evening. You can join us for coffee and dessert. Perhaps an after-dinner drink. Anything you wish to discuss with me will be confidential…you know, client-attorney privilege. Would that work for you?"

"Yes, I suppose it would. Eight o'clock?"

"Yes. My secretary will give you the address and basic directions. My home is not difficult to find."

****

"Are you sure you want me to stay for your meeting with Pollack?" Jake Lomax asked.

"Yeah, I'd like a second set of ears to be sure he's on the up and up. He won't pull any shenanigans with an attorney present."

"Does he know I'm Audrey's attorney and not yours?"

"I may be signing a client agreement with you before the evening's over, Jake."

The doorbell rang. Audrey answered it, welcomed Harry Pollack into her home, and escorted him to the dining room table where Michael and Jake were sitting. Michael introduced himself and then Jake. All three men shook hands.

"Coffee or brandy?" Michael asked.

"Whatever you're having," Pollack said.

"High test or decaf?" Audrey asked. "Cream and sugar?"

"High test. Black, please."

When Harry Pollack had been given his coffee and a piece of pecan pie, Michael got down to business. "You asked for this meeting, Mr. Pollack. How can I help you?"

"Call me 'Harry,' please."

Michael nodded.

Pollack swallowed a piece of pecan pie and chased it with a sip of coffee. "First, on behalf of the State's Republican party, permit me to apologize for pulling your name from candidacy for the State Supreme Court of Appeals when you were arrested on that trumped up rape charge. Party leaders were concerned your arrest would enable the Democrat to walk into the judgeship, sort of 'no contest.' That's why they replaced you with Christine Massullo."

"You're the party leader. Did you agree with the sentiment of the other officers?" Jake asked.

Pollack hung his head, causing his double chin to protrude on both sides of his cheeks. He loosened his red, white, and blue tie. "Yes, I'm embarrassed to say I did. I was wrong. I was thinking of the best interest of the party and not of the State."

"So, how can I be of service to you today, Harry?" Michael asked.

"It hasn't hit the papers yet…probably because the Democrats haven't gotten wind of it…but as soon as they do, Christine will be toast."

Michael and Jake both leaned forward in their chairs.

"Her husband was arrested in Beckley last night. He was in a motel room with a seventeen-year-old girl. They checked in as father and daughter. Apparently, they got drunk and when he fell asleep, she went swimming in the motel pool in her bra and undies." He looked at Audrey. "I apologize for mentioning women's unmentionables, ma'am."

Audrey nodded and smiled.

"They found half an ounce of cocaine in the room. When questioned by arresting officers, the young lady in question admitted to having snorted cocaine and having sex with Mr. Massullo that evening. Apparently, they've had an on-going relationship since she was sixteen, maybe even fifteen. This revelation will kill Christine's chances of being elected. The Democrat simply will be handed the judgeship."

Audrey noticed Pollack's coffee cup was nearly empty. "More coffee, Harry?"

He nodded and then he continued while Audrey filled his cup. "We know the Conservatives have never doubted you and have not removed your name from the ballot. If we Republicans are to make any changes to the ballot, we need to notify the Election Commission by Wednesday of next week—before the ballots go to the printer."

"So, you're asking Michael for permission to reinstate him as the Republican candidate and for him to re-launch a campaign at this late date?" Jake Lomax asked. "It's only three weeks until election day."

"You put two and two together pretty quickly, Mr. Lomax." Pollack stuffed another piece of pie into his mouth.

Audrey held up the coffee pot, but Pollack waved her off politely. She set the pot down and looked at her husband. "Are you ready to put yourself through a few weeks of no-sleep campaigning in order to have your name smeared with more mud than is already hanging off it? How can you expect to win with so little time between now and Election Day?"

Jake nodded. "If you do this, Michael, the

Democrats will have a heyday with your recent arrest and with the on-again off-again treatment you've received from the Republican Party. Their negative campaigning will be horrific. You and Audrey will have to grow very thick skin and prepare yourselves for a brutal onslaught."

Michael turned to Pollack. "What's your plan, Harry?"

"Assuming you give us the go-ahead, we'll try to get out front of the Musullo story. We'll say Christine has stepped down for personal reasons and she has recommended you be reinstated as the best individual to represent the State Republicans as appellate judge. This approach will help her save face and will encourage her loyal supporters to vote for you, instead."

Michael looked at Audrey, who nodded her head. "I'll support you fully," she said. "It's the way it should have been before that cow in New York tried to ruin you. I'll bet anything the Democrats put her up to it."

Jake Lomax smiled. "I like the fight you two have within you. No putting either of you down, no matter how much the opposition tries." He pointed at Audrey. "You're going to be on the campaign trail as much as Michael is, you know, going to women's groups all across the voting district to support his candidacy."

Audrey nodded.

"Then I can tell the Republican Party to move forward with reinstating you as our candidate?" Pollack asked.

"Tell them you were able to convince me that I was West Virginia's best hope."

"Thanks, Michael. And thank you, too, Mrs. Agosta. We'll get a press conference together for tomorrow. You'll both have to be there, right on the front steps of the State Capitol. I'll let you know what time."

Chapter 39

Margo dialed the cell phone number her sister Darla had given her when she unexpectedly visited two weeks before, after not talking with Margo for more than ten years. The phone rang six times before Darla answered.

After cool, but cordial hellos, Margo got down to business. "You and I need to talk, Darla. I got dragged down to the Willow Falls police department and was given the third degree on account of you. Now I want you to fess up and tell me what the hell is going on."

"You didn't tell no cops I was asking about what they found, did you?"

"No, I protected your butt, but now they suspect me of killing some guy they dug up in the garage at the abandoned house. Who was the guy you killed?"

Darla sounded sarcastic over the phone. "Really? Now why would you suspect me of killing some dude? Are you sure he was murdered? Was he shot or stabbed?"

Margo's voice was trembling with anger. "How would *I* know how he died? I didn't do it. And you know how they traced him back to me? It was my leather jacket. You stole my freaking leather jacket, you bitch. What kind of big sister sets her little sister up for a murder charge?"

Darla slammed the phone down. Then she took it

off the receiver so it would not ring when Margo called her back. She grabbed her purse, hopped into her car, and drove across town.

Margo was still fuming when her doorbell rang. She pulled back her living room curtains and saw Darla's car in her driveway. She stormed to her door and opened it. "How dare you hang up on me?"

Darla looked annoyed. "Are you gonna let me in or not? I've got a lot to tell you."

Margo let Darla pass into her foyer, then she looked up and down the neighborhood street before pulling her head back in and closing her door.

"Into the kitchen," Margo ordered.

"You got a beer?"

Margo poured Darla a jelly glass of Chardonnay. "That's going to have to do. You don't like Henry's beer, anyway."

Darla drank the entire glass and then held it out for a refill. Margo begrudgingly complied.

"Why did you kill the guy? And why did you bury my jacket with him?"

"Let's start with your jacket. Yeah, I took it from your closet one afternoon when you weren't home. It was cold and my old K-Mart nylon jacket looked like crap. It was dirty and needed washing, but I wasn't allowed to touch the washer, so I borrowed your jacket. I had a date, it was cold outside, and your jacket was 'there' so I took it and marched right out the door."

"What happened to it? Did you sell it or something?"

Darla scraped a speck of dried food from Margo's kitchen table. "No, I had a date. He was a gangbanger they called 'Johnny Pie.' He was a cool dresser and he always carried a biscuit. I was enamored with him. He was so bad."

"What's a biscuit?" Margo asked.

"A gun, L'il Sis. Sometimes he carried a nine, but usually a biscuit. A biscuit ain't nothing special...they're unmarked. You could buy 'em for less than ten dollars on the street back then."

Darla seemed to enjoy teaching her little sister some lingo and telling Margo about her gangbanger love interest. She took a long swallow of wine and then started again. "Johnny Pie and me, we just walked and talked, then he sprang for dinner at PopEye's. We sat on a picnic bench outside, and he was rubbin' his leg against mine while we ate and we was flirtin' with each other out in the cold."

Margo saw Darla's wine glass was almost empty, so she pulled the cork from the bottle of chardonnay and filled it again. She hoped it would continue to loosen Darla's tongue.

"So, Johnny Pie takes me to the WFC spot and introduces me around. I was feeling real special."

"What's WFC?"

"Where we lived, stupid. 'Willow Falls Clan.'" Darla adjusted her rump on the dark pine chair she was sitting on. "So, we drank some beer and Jack and then he lights up a joint and we got high. Then he shows me to their special place, a room with a couple of mattresses. I let him do me right there, first date. First time, no less."

"You barely knew him, Darla. How could you do that?"

"I wasn't happy at home, and he made me happy that night, so I sort of thanked him that way. I don't know. It jus' seemed right. Besides, I was sort of high."

Margo was starting to feel sorry for her sister. Darla couldn't have been more than sixteen when this event in her life happened. It was her first time with a man, and that was why she remembered it so clearly.

"So, why are you telling me all this, Darla?"

"Because I was telling you about your leather jacket." She took the last swig of wine and held her glass out.

Margo filled it and then threw the empty wine bottle into the kitchen trash can.

Darla took a small sip of wine. "Johnny Pie kept your leather jacket as a trophy for taking my virginity. He asked if he could have it, and it wasn't mine, so I didn't give a rat's ass about it, not really. I mean, you and I were barely speaking back then."

Darla drank more wine. "Johnny Pie and I were a number for a couple of months. I let him do me a couple of times a week." Her expression changed to remorse. "One day I come to see him, and he was in the special room with some other girl, a black one who was older than me. I screamed at him, and he screamed back at me. He threw the jacket at me and tol' me to get out, so I did."

"But you didn't give my jacket back to me."

"No, maybe I should have, but I guess I didn't. It sort of became the reward I'd give to any guy who would go steady with me. He could wear 'my' jacket as long as we was sleeping together and he was faithful just to me. Whenever we broke up, I'd take the jacket back and move along to the next guy."

"Next guy?"

"Yeah. After Johnny Pie was Mescal. They said he

was a rising star with the Mexicans. Their place was just three blocks from our home, so close I could be there in a couple of minutes. Daddy didn't even know they was there. The sign in the window said it was vacuum cleaner repair."

Margo nodded. "Yes, I remember Mescal's name because it was so strange when I first heard it. Is he the one who got you pregnant?"

"Oh no. He always used protection. Said I was too young. Jail bait." Darla finished the last of her wine. "I was with Mescal for four months, then I was with Juaquin for three or four months, and then there was Poco. Poco and I were together for a year and a half. I thought we was gonna get married, but he dumped me for another white girl from high school." Darla paused to catch her breath. "Then there was Miguel. He's the one who got me pregnant the first time. Once I got pregnant, he stayed with me 'til Julio was born, but he wouldn't marry me. Said I'd been with too many guys."

"And each of these guys wore my leather jacket when they were going steady with you?"

"Yeah, they did." Darla hung her head. "You know, when I hear myself tell my story, I been with a lot of guys, and most of them treated me bad. Mom and Pop were right about trying to live the good life. I wish I had been smart enough to listen to them,"

A horn honked outside, sending Margo to the door to see who was there. It was Henry and he was upset because Darla's car was blocking his access to the garage. Margo signaled to him to wait a moment, then she hurried back into the kitchen.

"Henry's home and wants into the garage, so you need to leave."

"But, there's more to tell you."

"I don't have any more wine, and Henry isn't going to be happy that you're here. How about we meet again in a few days, and you can finish your story. I'm less angry now about my jacket than I was, but I still have a few questions to ask you. And I still have to get the police off my back."

Darla said goodbye, strutted out the front door, and climbed awkwardly into her car. Henry pulled out of the driveway so she could exit. When she backed onto the street, he gave her a loud and long blast on his horn because she nearly struck his front bumper with her car. She flipped him off, put her car in drive, and left him in a cloud of oil-rich exhaust.

"What was *she* doing here?" Henry asked when he came into the kitchen from the garage. Margo could see he was irritated Darla had been inside his home.

"I think she's the key to finding out who the guy in the garage was, and maybe who buried him."

"Well, call that detective, what's his name, and have him pull it out of her."

"She isn't going to tell him anything she knows. She'd rather go to jail than rat out somebody, even somebody she doesn't like."

"You mean she'd rather see you go to jail than to let the police learn the truth about the second skeleton."

"I won't let that happen, Henry. I won't let that happen."

Chapter 40

I called Helen and arranged for her to accompany me to Grace Street, where we drove slowly along three blocks of dilapidated two-family rentals until we came to a yellow one with red shutters. It was time to interview the little sister of the guy who gave her up during my interview with the Mexicans.

"This gotta be the place," Helen said.

I pulled over and parallel parked between a fifteen-year-old Pontiac Lemans with a peeling white vinyl top and a panel truck with rotted-out quarter panels.

"They don't upgrade their wheels too often in this neighborhood," I said.

"Most of these vehicles are probably homes for the peeps who can't afford to live in the high rises."

The QVC channel was blasting from the downstairs apartment when we knocked on its green wooden door. An obese black woman in a flower-print muumuu opened the door and greeted us. "You from the Adventists?"

I flashed my badge. "Are you Jasmine Goins?"

"What you want with her? She don't do nothin' would bring no cops down here to this neighborhood."

"Can you tell us when she'll be home?" Helen asked.

"She home now. Hear that racket from her tape player? Why you think I got the TV on so loud? Can't hear nothing over that loud stuff she play upstairs."

Helen thanked the woman and then she and I rang the bell for the upstairs apartment. Nothing. Helen rang it again. The loud noise coming from upstairs quieted. Helen rang the bell a third time.

A voice from upstairs yelled, "That you, Kimeesha? Come on up."

I looked at Helen, who shrugged, opened the door, and climbed to the second floor. I was right behind her. At the top, Helen knocked three times.

The door opened. A middle-aged woman in a white bra and pink underwear quickly jumped back. "You ain't Kimeesha." She covered herself with a beach towel printed with pink and aquamarine seahorses.

Helen showed her badge. "We need to talk with you, Jasmine. You're not in trouble, but we're hoping you can help us out with a case we're investigating.

Jasmine asked permission to change into some clothes. Helen nodded. She disappeared into one of the two bedrooms in the apartment. I drifted around the kitchen, looking at the Cheerios Jasmine probably had eaten for breakfast and the black coffee she had left in a plain white mug. It was still warm. Her apartment was outfitted in inexpensive furniture. I had not expected anything different. There was no evidence of alcohol or drugs. I had not expected that either.

A minute later Jasmine came out of her bedroom wearing black tights and a sleeveless yellow sweatshirt top. A man's silver ring with a square black stone dangled from her neck on a long silver chain. I figured she was going steady with someone. She was barefoot, and her hair was still damp, with minute diamonds of water sparkling in the mid-morning light. Her eyes were bright, and the crow's feet near them were the only indication she was older than thirty.

I felt it best for Helen to interview Jasmine, especially since they already had established a relationship of mutual respect over the phone. And especially since Jasmine and Helen shared the same race and gender.

"We're here because your name came up in an investigation of a possible murder," Helen said.

Jasmine's face contorted at the thought that she could be connected to a murder. "How does this involve me?"

"That's what we're trying to determine."

Helen motioned to a stuffed chair as if to ask if she could sit. Jasmine nodded. Helen sat, but I stood behind Jasmine just in case she tried to bolt out the door.

"We're sorry to interrupt your morning, especially since you're expecting Kimeesha," Helen said. "We'll try not to stay too long."

Jasmine nodded and sat upright.

"We're investigating the discovery of a skeleton. It was buried in a shallow grave behind a vacant house on Spencer Street."

Jasmine nodded. She slumped her shoulders slightly.

"From one of the people we interviewed last week, we learned you were there when the body was buried. We'd like you to confirm or deny that, and then tell us what happened and who was there."

"You said I wasn't in no trouble."

"You're not in any trouble. We need to know what went down and who was involved. That's all."

"I know what you're talking about, I mean the

body and all. I was there when the body was buried, but it weren't no murder."

Helen crossed her legs and relaxed in her chair. "Tell us about it, Jasmine."

"It was about five or six years ago. I'd have to think awhile before I could tell you exactly when. Me and Darla and Squiggles and Nadine was snooping around the house where Darla's sister L'il Margo used to meet her white guy, the one what was in the newspaper story a few months back. I don't know if they really did what the paper said they was up to cause I never seen her do it, but Darla said L'il Margo did. We went into the empty house and walked around the rooms and saw the mattress where they did what they did. And then, when we went outside, we went into the garage 'cause there was this awful stink coming from it. We found this guy all puffed up with black lips and bulging eyes and a swollen belly. Maybe I seen him before but I ain't sure. We wasn't sure what to do with him, but we decided to bury him. They sent me outside to keep watch. I closed the garage door and waited outside while they dug a hole and buried him. He was dead when they buried him, the girls who dug the hole. My job was to stand outside and watch for cops or others who might happen to come by during the burial ceremony."

"You called it a 'ceremony.' Why's that?"

"The other girls sang a song after they buried him. How it go? Oh yeah, 'Amazin' Grace.'"

"Who's idea was it to bury the body?" I asked.

Jasmine looked up at me. "I ain't sure. I think maybe it was Darla's idea. You'll have to ask her. I'm pretty sure it was Darla who first suggested it."

"Do you know the name of the guy they buried?"

"A few times they talk about it, you know, later on…a couple of the girls called him 'Big Wax'"

"Are you sure about that?" I asked.

"Yessir, they called him Big Wax."

Chapter 41

Margo heard squealing brakes outside her home at eleven in the morning on Tuesday. Peering out her living room curtains, she saw Darla's car in her driveway. She hurried to her front door and opened it before Darla rang the doorbell.

"Good morning, L'il Sis," Darla said as she walked into the Lumpas' foyer. "You gonna make me lunch?"

Margo walked into the kitchen ahead of Darla and opened the refrigerator door. "Bologna or olive loaf? White or whole wheat? Mayonnaise or just mustard?"

"You know me, L'il Sis. Nothing fancy. Make it bologna and mayo on white bread. Got any beer?"

"Yeah, I bought a six pack of Bud for when you came back. Thought you might."

Margo handed Darla a beer and then turned to make her sandwich.

Darla popped the top and chugged a third of the can. "So where did I leave off last time?"

"You were telling me about the guy who got you pregnant the first time."

"Miguel?"

"Yeah. You said he stayed with you for a year and a half, or at least until the baby was born."

"That's right. You got a good memory, girl."

"Call it shock effect. I didn't know anything about what you were doing as a kid. I was just your annoying little sister, and you didn't tell me much. What you laid on me the other day was a lot to absorb."

"It felt good to tell somebody about it. That's why I'm back. I want to feel good some more."

Margo slid a red, white, and blue paper plate with the bologna sandwich across the table to Darla. Then she plopped an unopened bag of potato chips next to the plate. "So, what happened when Julio was born?"

"I was living at Squiggles' place. Her momma was good to me 'cause I was pregnant. Let me stay 'til Julio was born, too. Then she asked me to leave. She was polite and everything, but she tol' me she couldn't stand his crying at all hours of the night. She gave him a teaspoon of bourbon with sugar to make him sleep. It worked, but I knew it weren't no good for Julio."

"Why didn't you ask Mom and Dad if you could come home?"

"Never would have. Went to Social Services and got a small apartment for free. Got milk, cheese, and peanut butter from WIC. Got food stamps and Dependent Children money. I guess I got by okay, but it was a hard life."

"I'll bet."

"And the County was messed up, too. Whenever I got a part-time job, they cut my monthly check. Why they do that? Never could get ahead for being pushed back down by the man."

Margo wanted to learn more about her sister's life, especially if she could get Darla to reveal what happened to the black leather jacket with the chrome stars. "So, did you date anyone after Julio's father?"

"Well, I quit hanging with the Mexicans and found old friends among the Keyboard Clan. You know, high school friends."

"How did they get that name?"

"From that song. They're not just black guys like most Clan chapters. They're both black and white, like on a piano. You know, like the song goes."

"Ebony and Ivory?"

"Yeah, that's it."

Darla had eaten half her sandwich and finished her first beer, so Margo handed her another. Darla popped the top and a small head of suds filled the can lid. She licked it off.

"So, I hung with them for most of my adult life. I'd go steady with one guy, then move to the next. I'm embarrassed to tell you, but sometimes I'd sleep with two or three different guys on the same weekend. It was about two years later when I got pregnant again. It was an accident. Ran out of birth control pills and the Planned Parenthood was closed when I went there, so I just risked it. Guess I shouldn't have. And that's how Lisamona came to be."

Margo hadn't met either of Darla's children. "Her name sounds like 'Mona Lisa'"

"It 'sposed to, but I turned it backwards so she unique, you know?"

"Who's her father?"

"Don't really know. Could be any one of the Clan guys. Maybe two or three of them are her father. They don't care. They all help out. They all come to see her on her birthday. She likes it. She's twelve now."

"Did they all wear my jacket?"

"Only the ones I went steady with, just like with the Mexicans."

Margo pushed for the answer to the question which

had been eating at her for the past few weeks. "How did my jacket end up in the grave with the man in the garage?"

"Me, and Squiggles, and Jasmine, and Nadine, we was looking in the house where you and that white boy used to get it on. We was outside and smelled something awful coming from the garage. We opened the door and found this guy dead. I recognized him. It was Big Wax, and he was dead. Maybe three or four days dead."

"Why didn't you call the cops?"

"Why didn't you call the cops when your l'il baby was dead, Sis? We did the same as you. Nobody want no trouble, no police snooping around asking questions of all the gang bangers. No gang bangers going to war 'cause somebody killed one of their own. Nadine said it best we just bury him, so we did."

"And my jacket?"

"I'm coming to it. So, we sent Jasmine outside to watch for cops and we dug a hole, not too deep, but deep enough to roll him into. When we pushed him in, he plopped on his back and was looking straight up with those big brown eyes just staring up at us. I couldn't throw no dirt into those open eyes. Didn't want no ghost coming after me in my sleep. Only thing I had was the jacket, so I threw it over his face before we shoveled dirt onto it. That's how it got there, honest."

Darla's story made sense to Margo, so she accepted it. At least for the time being. But there were so many questions to ask. Darla said she had recognized the dead man, but she did not say the other girls recognized him. How did she know him? How did he die?

Margo's cell phone rang. It was Henry. He was on

his way home from school for a quick lunch and to change his clothes. One of the girls in his eleven o'clock Biology lab had thrown up on his pants and shoes during cat dissection. "Could you make me a quick sandwich?" he asked.

Margo hustled Darla out the door with promises to meet again soon, and maybe to meet her kids, Julio and Lisamona. She was not sure she wanted to open that door, but maybe the kids needed to know they had an aunt. Maybe they needed to know they had family beyond the men in the Keyboard Clan. Maybe they needed to see if they followed a different path, they could have a better life than the one their mother had suffered. Maybe. If it was not already too late.

Chapter 42

Michael Agosta's suit against Albany County, New York, was filed within five days of his acquittal on rape charges. His New York attorney Lester Brockbank sued for false arrest, frivolous unfounded charges, defamation of character, and loss of income. He also asked the court to make the County pay all legal fees associated with the defense, since it appeared the plaintiff was unable to do so in a timely manner.

Michael never had to appear in court; however, he had to write a witnessed deposition outlining the burdens the case had laid upon himself and his family. Brockbank argued the preliminary case in Michael's absence, estimating Michael's loss of income at three million dollars over twenty years. He asked ten million dollars for defamation of character, especially since the case caused Michael to be dropped as a candidate for West Virginia Supreme Court of Appeals. And he argued that the District Attorney's penalty for false arrest under unfounded charges should be worth at least another five million dollars. "No district attorney should arrest any individual without proper grounds and evidence," he proclaimed.

Under pressure from the judge, before a trial date was set, the insurance attorneys representing Albany County met with Brockbank in his office. The lead attorney for the insurance company was a thin man with a slight nervous tick in his neck. Brockbank had to look away as he spoke to avoid staring at him. "We're prepared to settle out of court for three million dollars," the lead attorney said. "A man of Mr. Agosta's education and experience will find a higher paying job in short order. However, our offer includes one million in lost wages, one million for false arrest, and one million for defamation of character. It's a fair amount, and he should be satisfied with that."

Brockbank smiled. "My client has nothing left to lose. His name has been all over the television news on the east coast, and his enemies in the West Virginia press have ravaged him for weeks. He doubts he'll ever be able to work again, except maybe as a volunteer at Legal Aid. He feels the eighteen million we're asking for is fair, and probably too little, given the personal and professional damages he's suffered. However, in order to avoid further embarrassment to Albany County and the County's D.A., he is willing to settle for fifteen million dollars."

"I don't have the authority to go that high," the lead lawyer said.

"Then what's your max?" Brockbank asked. "It had better be at least twelve million dollars, or we'll see you in court and a jury can decide how much compensation he should be awarded. As you know, juries in New York have been very generous of late."

The lead attorney asked for a brief recess while he called the home office. Brockbank escorted him and his two trainees to a private conference room. As he was closing the door, Brockbank saw the trainees wandering the room with hand-held meters, searching for cameras and electronic listening devices. He hadn't expected that, but big insurance companies distrust everything and everyone.

Five minutes later, the three attorneys re-entered Brockbank's office. The lead attorney handed Brockbank a folded piece of paper. "That's as high as we're willing to go."

Brockbank unfolded the paper, where the figure $11,500,000 had been scrawled. "I think I can get my client to agree to this figure."

"Good. We want him to sign a non-disclosure agreement and we want your agreement that you won't fight an order to seal the court records."

"Agreed," Brockbank said. "Have your people draft the necessary paperwork and notify the judge of our tentative agreement. As soon as I've read and agreed to the terms, Mr. Agosta will sign the documents and you can go home."

"Thank you, Mr. Brockbank. It's been a pleasure."

"Yes, it has."

****

Brockbank dialed Michael's home telephone number in West Virginia. Audrey answered.

"I have good news for Michael. Is he there?"

"Yes, he is," Audrey replied, "but he's really tired. After work today, he was interviewed by two different television talk shows for the evening news, and he's been preparing his speech for a rally at the Canaan Valley Conference Center in Davis this weekend. The pace of the campaign is accelerating."

"I won't take long, and my news may take a little weight off his shoulders."

"Okay, I'll get him." Audrey covered the receiver with her palm. "It's Lester Brockbank. He says it's good news."

Michael's voice came on the phone. "Hey, Les. I'm so glad you're not another reporter."

"You'll be even happier in a moment, Michael."

"Whatcha got for me?"

"We settled out of court today. Albany County's insurance attorney approved eleven and a half."

"Million?"

"Yeah, million."

"That's way more than I thought they'd go. I guess I have to do some soul searching to figure out what to do with the money."

"Well, don't forget I get a third," Brockbank said. "I may go to Disney World."

Michael laughed. "I would never forget your share." He turned his face from the phone and coughed. "I just want to thank you for everything you've done for me—you know, the advice and counsel in New York and now this settlement. I thought we might get five, but never figured on more than seven."

"Don't forget there's a non-disclosure agreement. You and Audrey can't tell anyone how much we got from the County, or you'll lose it all."

"I understand, and I'll ensure Audrey complies. When she's asked about the settlement, I'm sure she'll remember that saying anything will cost her close to nine million dollars. No woman wants to lose that kind of spending power."

Brockbank laughed. "You're probably right about that." He paused, then added, "Listen. Get some sleep, Michael. You want to be in top form at Canaan Valley."

"Yeah. Thanks so much for the good news. Maybe it's a harbinger of things to come."

Chapter 43

"This place is better to meet, don't you think?" Darla asked. "At least we don't got to worry that Henry will walk in on us here."

They were sitting in a booth at Verrigni's at Darla's suggestion. But they had to speak in low voices so as not to be overheard. Margo sprang for one donut each, a hot chocolate, and a coffee for Darla. She threw her change into a jar which had a black and white photo of a crippled child taped to it.

"So, before Henry interrupted us last time, you told me when you and the other girls found the body, you recognized the dead guy in the garage," Margo said, stirring her paper cup full of hot chocolate with a wooden spoon.

Darla blew on her coffee. "Ain't the milk and sugar supposed to cool it down?"

Margo shrugged and waited for Darla's answer.

"Yeah, I recognized him all right. I slept with him a few times, not because I wanted to, but because no other females was around and I'd serve the purpose. I never gave him the jacket because we never went steady. Never would have with him, anyway."

Margo sipped her hot chocolate. White powdered sugar from her donut clung to her upper lip. "Why's that?"

"He was mean, Big Wax. With some men, it's all

about them. Big Wax was one of them. If he asked you to do something, you better do it or he hit you backhand with that ring on his pinkie finger. If he hit you just right, that ring would draw blood. And he'd cut you with a knife if you cussed him. He never hit me, but he yelled a lot, and he threw me around. Bruised my arms and legs. When he decided he wanted you, you better be willing 'cause he was going to do you whether you were ready or not. He hurt you that way too, tear you up if you weren't ready, if you know what I mean."

"You had to be happy to see him dead."

Darla nodded and blew on her coffee again. "Yeah, him being dead was a good thing for a lot of women."

"Did you kill him, Darla?"

Darla looked up as if Margo had pierced her heart with an ice pick. "I already told you I didn't do it. You're my l'il sis. I wouldn't lie to you. Don't you believe me?"

Margo pushed on. "Do you know who killed him?"

"I got suspicions, but I don't know for sure who done the deed. I mean, if a deed was really done. I wish I did know so's I could pat them on the back and shake their hand. But I didn't do it or help plan it or nothing. All I did is help dig the hole we rolled him into, and then throw dirt and leaves over his body…and your jacket." Darla slurped her coffee. "Wish the dogs had found him and dug him up, but that would never have happened because when we were finished, I closed the garage door and put a rusty nail in the hinge thing."

****

Margo left Verrigni's with Darla and dropped her on a corner near the barrio side of town. She would have driven Darla to her door, but Darla asked to be let out at the corner. So, Margo still didn't know where Darla lived, and she still had not met her niece and nephew.

On her way home, Margo's mind played over and over the information she had received from Darla during their three recent meetings. Clearly, Darla was suspicious Big Wax had been murdered in some way, and Darla was suspicious a specific person had "done the deed," but Darla was not forthcoming with the details of her suspicions. But that was Darla's M.O.— she always held back vital information and had been doing so since they were little girls.

As she passed by the Willow Falls Police Department, Margo did an unpredictable thing. She turned into the visitors' lot and went into the building.

I was at my desk when the desk sergeant called me to announce Mrs. Margo Lumpas was here to see me. You could have knocked me over with a feather.

"Please send her up."

After she was wanded by building security, Margo found her way to the third floor, where Helen Martin and I were waiting for her.

"I hope you don't mind my coming without an appointment," Margo said. She was dressed down: blue jeans, a pink sweatshirt top, and tennis shoes. Her hair was slightly unkempt.

"Are you here to make a confession?" Helen asked.

"Hardly. I've been doing your job and I'm here to report my findings."

"This should be interesting," Helen smirked.

I pointed to the chair across the desk from me. "Please sit down, Mrs. Lumpas."

Margo sat down and plopped her purse on my

desk. "So, here's what I have for you," she began. "I want to remind you I haven't seen my black leather motorcycle jacket in many years. It disappeared when I was in high school."

I nodded. "Do you mind if I tape this information?"

"If you must."

I opened my desk drawer and pulled out my small digital recorder, the same one I had used during previous interviews with Margo.

"Can I continue now?" she asked,

I nodded and pressed the "record" button.

"So, I haven't seen that jacket since I was a kid. It just disappeared. Well, recently I've been getting reacquainted with my estranged sister. Actually, she came to see *me* almost immediately after the newspaper ruined my life when it ran the story of my FF relationship with Michael Agosta."

"What's your sister's name?" Helen asked.

"Oh. Darla Borst. I don't think she's ever been married."

"Go on," I said, pointing at my recorder.

"So, Darla tells me she's the one who took my jacket, and some guy kept it after he took her virginity. Later, they had a fight, and he threw it at her. From there, every time she went steady with a guy, she let him wear the jacket. She hung with a Mexican gang for a while and then started hanging with the Clan. She has two kids, one by men in each gang."

"Where's this going, Mrs. Lumpas?" Helen asked.

Margo leaned forward. "To the point, when she and three other girls discovered the body in the garage, they dug a hole and buried it to avoid a gang war. Darla said she covered the cadaver's face with the jacket because she didn't want to be haunted by it."

"Are you saying Darla killed the guy?" I asked.

"No, not at all. I asked her that directly several times and she always denied it. I believe her. She can't be sure, but if it was a murder, she suspects a certain person might have done it."

"Who?" Helen asked.

Margo shrugged. "She wouldn't tell me."

"Did she identify the cadaver?"

"Yes, some guy called 'Big Wax.' I think he was affiliated with the Clan."

"Big Max?" I asked for verification.

"No. Big Wax, like floor wax."

"How did she know this guy?"

"She said he forced her to have sexual relations several times. That it was all about him, and if she resisted, he would backhand her and cut her face with his pinkie ring. He forced himself upon her several times."

Helen snorted and crossed her legs. "Sounds like some of the guys I've dated."

"I'm sorry," Margo said to her. "I guess some men are that way. I think you can spot some of them before they ever ask you out. They're certainly men to avoid."

Helen nodded. "Ain't that the truth."

"So, what do you want me to do with this information?" I asked. "Haul your sister in for interrogation?"

"No, please don't do that, or she'll never confide in me again. I just thought if you could find the other three women who helped bury Big Wax, maybe you could figure out who Darla suspects."

"Did she give you any names?" Helen asked.

"Yes, actually. I wrote them down as soon as she left." Margo pulled out a small piece of paper and read, "Squiggles and Jasmine, and Nadine."

I wrote the names down. "No last names?"

"No, but finding that stuff out is your job, isn't it?" Margo asked.

"He isn't much good at it," Helen said, "but I'll have them by tomorrow morning."

"Anything else?" I asked.

"That's all I can think of. I still have your card. I'll call you if I remember anything else."

"Thank you, Mrs. Lumpas," I said. "You've been extremely helpful. We'll keep you apprised of what we discover."

After Margo left, Helen was the first to speak. "We've already interviewed Jasmine. Same names she gave us. We've got to get her to give us access to the other two, Squiggles and Nadine."

"Yeah," I replied. "And she said Big Wax wore a pinkie ring. Is it at all suspicious his skeleton didn't have a pinkie finger?"

"Oooh, you're good, Jonesy."

Chapter 44

It was a cold and rainy Thursday morning when Helen drove across town to see Jasmine without calling ahead. As she pulled to a stop outside Jasmine's apartment, she looked up at Jasmine's picture window and saw her struggling with a young black man. She quickly got out of her car and ran through the rain to the stairway which ascended to Jasmine's front door.

As Helen neared the top of the stairs, the front door burst open, and the young black man charged out. Helen pulled her pistol from her hip. "Freeze."

The young man was so startled he yelped like a dog and tumbled down the stairs, bringing Helen with him. When they reached the bottom, Helen grabbed his hands and cuffed him. As she did, a silver necklace and a ring fell onto the bottom step from the man's right hand.

Jasmine appeared at the top of the stairs. "He got what's mine," she screamed. "Make him give it back."

Holding onto the assault suspect with her left hand, Helen raised her right and showed the necklace and ring to Jasmine. "Is this what he took?"

"Oh, thank you. Thank you. My papa gave it to me on his death bed."

Helen tilted her head in the direction of the young man in her grasp. "What's his name?

"He's Leroy, but the Clan call him L'il Pookey."

"Come get it, sweetheart. You lock up and come with me. You're gonna swear out an assault charge and we're gonna see L'il Pookey spends the night in the slammer."

Jasmine hurried down the stairs, took the necklace, and then ran back up to lock her apartment. While she was gone, Helen called for backup. A black and white city cruiser arrived in less than sixty seconds. Two officers, one white and one black, stepped out with authority.

"Take this bad boy back to the Department," Helen said. "I'll be booking him for assault and theft."

The white officer looked slovenly. His shirt was splattered with coffee stains, and his stomach hung over his belt as though his pants were three sizes too small. "You got a name, son?"

The kid spit blood onto the sidewalk. "L'il Pookey." His face was scraped, and his low rider jeans were torn at the knee from falling down the stairs. He was missing one tennis shoe.

The white officer's partner, a thin black patrolman whose uniform was impeccable, found the shoe and handed it to the kid. "He ain't no 'L'il Pookey.' His name is Leroy Barnes. He lives over on West Second Street with his mama. She's a social worker with the City. She's gonna whip the shit out of him for getting arrested." The patrolman looked at Leroy with his right palm extended. "Why you want to bring this misery down on your mama, son? She been good to you. Why you hanging with them Clan scum? They nothing but trouble."

The officers shoved Leroy into the back seat of their cruiser. "See you back at the ranch, Martin," the fat white patrolman said.

Jasmine came down the stairs in a yellow hooded raincoat and stood next to Helen while the officers left with Leroy in the back seat. As the cruiser accelerated forward, Leroy looked through the side window and flipped off Jasmine. Or maybe he flipped off Helen. Or both.

Helen opened her car door for Jasmine and then walked around and let herself in. Her tan wool sweater was soaked with rainwater and her gray slacks were streaked with mud. She fluffed her hair with her fingers, but it was matted. "I'm a mess," she said. "But let's go do what we have to do before I go home and change."

****

I joined Helen while she instructed Jasmine on how to fill out an official complaint form.

"Clan find out I do this, they come after me and hurt me," Jasmine said.

Helen gave her an alternate form.

Jasmine seemed confused. "What this one?"

"It's a crime witness form. You just write down what you saw me do, and I'll issue the formal complaint."

"You a cop. Can you really do that?"

"She can do it," I said,

Helen nodded and pointed at the form. "Just tell how you saw me apprehend a guy who had stolen some jewelry from a woman. Tell how you saw me arrest him and that the guy I arrested was, in fact, the guy who stole the jewelry. Then sign it. I'll take care of the rest on my Arresting Officer's Report."

When Jasmine had finished writing her eyewitness

account, Helen took her to her desk and asked her to sit.

I followed. "You want a soda or a coffee?" I asked.

Jasmine shook her head.

"I need some additional help from you, Jasmine," Helen said.

Jasmine nodded and sat up straight, but apprehensive.

"I need to find your old friends Squiggles and Nadine. Do you ever see them anymore?"

Jasmine just stared at Helen and slowly slumped in her chair.

"I need to know their real names and where they live. Can you give me that information?"

"Why you want that?"

"I'm still working on Big Wax's death. The coroner needs to know if he was murdered of if he overdosed on something, that's all."

"They be real mad at me if I tell you where they is."

"Does it really make a difference?" I asked. "Would they come to your defense if you were charged with 'accessory to murder'?"

Jasmine looked up at me and then shot Helen a mean look. "You said I wasn't in no trouble.'

"You aren't. Detective Jones is just frustrated because you're reluctant to give us their real names and addresses, especially when I helped you this morning. You still have your necklace and your father's ring, don't you?"

Jasmine looked down at the floor. "Nadine is Nadine Washington. Squiggles is Kameesha Smith. I don't know their addresses."

"I have to drive you home, anyway," Helen said.

"Can you show us where they live, honey?"

Jasmine nodded. A tear ran down her cheek. Helen handed her a tissue.

Ten minutes later, Helen, Jasmine, and I were in Helen's car. Helen was driving and I was sitting beside Jasmine in the back seat, while she gave Helen directions through the minority neighborhood. The rain had stopped, but the streets were still wet and large puddles of water sat at the edge of almost every intersection.

"Slow down right here," Jasmine said. She pointed down the street. "See the brown two story with the green shutters?"

"Number 3412?" I asked.

"That be Nadine's house. Downstairs."

I wrote Nadine's address in my notepad.

We drove three blocks and made a right-hand turn. Jasmine seemed confused. "Squiggles home be here the other day. It gone."

"What do you mean?" I asked. "How could it be gone?"

"She live in a white van. It gone."

"There's two hundred white vans in Willow Falls, Jasmine," I replied.

"Hers got a green back bumper and the side got a big black square where her boyfriend painted over the picture of the lobster."

"You mean the van belonged to a fish store before?" Helen asked.

"Yes, ma'am. She live with Jeremy in that van. They fix it up real nice."

"Jeremy who? What's his last name?"

"I don't know his last name, but he work for

you…you know, the police department."

Helen shot me a quick look. I nodded.

"Thanks, Jasmine," Helen said. "We're gonna take you home now."

"Yes, ma'am."

Chapter 45

We dropped Jasmine at her home. Then Helen and I doubled back to Nadine's home at 3412 Albany Street. While Helen drove, I mumbled something aloud.

"What'd you say, Jonesy?"

I released my seatbelt, shifted my weight, and then snapped my seatbelt again. "I said, 'Jasmine is hiding something.' We gotta squeeze these other two women until one of them gives us something to crack this case."

"Yeah, Jasmine ain't telling us everything she knows, that's for sure."

Helen hit her turn signal and pulled to a stop in front of Nadine's house. As she did, a middle-aged black woman exited the door and hurried west along the sidewalk.

"Follow her, Helen. I'll bet you anything that's Nadine, and Jasmine just warned her we were coming."

Helen backed out of the parking space and followed the woman. It was easy to keep an eye on her because she was wearing purple leotards with a paisley print and a blaze orange jacket. A navy-blue wool stocking cap was pulled down over her ears. She was moving quickly, not quite running, but she certainly was not going to see her dentist.

Nadine walked two blocks and then suddenly stopped, leaned against a thirty-six-inch steel exhaust pipe which was bolted to the side of a brown brick building, and lit a cigarette. Helen parked half a block past her, and then she and I got out and walked casually in her direction.

Nadine looked up and saw us coming. She threw her cigarette in our direction and then took off running back toward her apartment. Helen and I pursued her. Well, I sped ahead because Helen was wearing clogs and they are not intended for a full sprint pursuit.

I caught up with Nadine about half a block from her apartment. I grabbed the back of her jacket and yelled, "Stop. You've got no place to run." Nadine tried to unzip her jacket, but the zipper caught in the flap of material which covered it. She gave up trying to escape.

Helen caught up about ten seconds later. "Nadine Washington?"

"Who wants to know?"

"Willow Falls Police," Helen huffed. "You're pretty fast for a middle-aged woman."

"I coulda run faster if I had me some tennis shoes."

"Why were you running at all?" I asked, snapping a handcuff onto her left wrist.

Nadine pulled her free hand away. "Why you arresting me? I ain't done nothing wrong."

I snapped the free cuff onto my own wrist. "There. Now you can't run anywhere unless you can drag me along."

We escorted her back to Helen's car, Nadine pulling against the handcuffs most of the way. I unsnapped the cuff from my wrist and snapped it onto the side mirror of Helen's car.

Helen gave Nadine a stern look. "Now don't you be trying to pull that mirror off my car. All we wanna do is talk with you."

Nadine rolled her eyes. "Why you think I want to talk to you police?"

"Because you may have some information to help us solve a case," I said.

Nadine jiggled her cuffed hand and saw there was no use in trying to break free.

"Did Jasmine call you just before we arrived?" Helen asked

"I don't know no Jasmine."

"I'll take that as a yes," Helen said.

"What you want?"

"Tell us everything you know about Big Wax," I said.

Nadine put her right hand in her jacket pocket and pulled out a tissue. "He dead," she said, wiping sweat from her forehead.

"Did you ever date him?" I asked.

"Nobody date Big Wax. He never ask nobody on a date. He just tell you he want to get it on and if you got no place to run, you better let him do it right then."

"Tell us about him, Nadine," Helen asked nicely. "Maybe I can get Detective Jones to remove your handcuff."

"His daddy was Mexican Banditos, but Big Wax was Clan. I was one of four girls…we was just girls back then. Didn't know no better…We hung with him for a couple of months. He was mean to us all. Hit me a lot. Any time I came to the crib, he took any money and any dope I had on me. Anything we got that he want, he just take it and laugh if we get upset."

I could see Nadine was going to answer our questions, so I unlocked the handcuff from her left wrist. She rubbed her wrist with her right hand.

"Do you know how Big Wax died?" I asked.

"I don't know for sure. Word is he was shootin' up stuff with some guys. He just died right there. Least they found him dead when they woke up."

"Did you bury his body?" Helen asked.

"Oooh, God, the memory of his body, all blowed up and dark purple like that. It can give you nightmares."

Helen waited for a few seconds and then asked her question again. "Did you bury his body?"

"Yes," Nadine said. "You probably already know who I was with. Jasmine wanted to go see the house where Darla's little sister used to do that white boy. So, we do that. Then we go outside and smell something miserable. Darla opened the door to the garage, and there he was, all puffed up like a balloon. I wanted to vomit. We sent Jasmine out to keep watch, and me, and Darla, and Squiggles, we dug a hole and pushed him in."

"Did you put a blanket or anything over him before you covered him in dirt?"

"Darla, she took off her jacket and threw it over his face."

"Did Big Wax have all his fingers?" I asked.

"Didn't look at that. Just wanted him buried and gone. Darla said we should bury him on account he be dead would cause a gang war."

"Did Big Wax wear any chains or other jewelry?" Helen asked.

"Onliest thing I remember was the ring he took from Jasmine. Like I said, he take your stuff and laugh when you want it back. He took Jasmine's ring, the one she wear around her neck, and he put it on his little finger and wouldn't give it back."

"He never gave it back?" I asked.

"Not that I know of. He had that ring on his finger for as long as I can remember. Sometimes Jasmine come into a room, and he just put his hand up in the air and wiggle his finger. When she get mad at him, he just laugh."

"Thank you, sweetheart," Helen said. "You got no reason to run from the police. I know you don't believe this, but we *are* your friends."

Chapter 46

Jeremy was sitting with Francine Roberts in the Forensics unit when Helen and I came for a visit. Francine looked up and greeted us just as I started to knock on her office door. Jeremy stood to leave the room, thinking we needed a word with Francine.

"Don't go yet, Jeremy," I said. Then I turned to Francine. "Can we speak with Jeremy alone for a few minutes?"

"He isn't in trouble with the law, is he?" Francine asked.

"No, but he may be able to help us solve the case that had you guys digging for bones on Clement Street," Helen replied.

"I'll bet you've got a good bowling average," I said to Jeremy, "the way you were handling that skull."

Jeremy laughed. "It's best to hold them that way, so you don't mess up any places where the skull has been damaged by a bullet or a hammer. Francine taught me that."

"Gotcha," I replied. The technique probably made sense, in a sordid sort of way.

Francine gave us her office and walked out into the lab, where she began sorting and cleaning the tools of her trade.

"How can I help you?" Jeremy asked.

"Do you know a woman named Kameesha Smith?"

I asked.

Jeremy pulled his head back. "What's this about? Is she in trouble?"

"Squiggles was one of four girls who buried the body you dug up on Clement Street," Helen said.

"How do you know that name? I thought I was the only person who calls her 'Squiggles.' That's a pet name I gave her, just a few months ago."

"I think everyone calls her that. Jonesy here is the only person who calls her 'Kameesha,' "

Jeremy sat down in Francine's desk chair. "You don't say? She was actually involved in a case you're investigating?"

"Yeah," I said. "Got to know though...do you drive a white van with a green rear bumper. You know, an old fish delivery truck?"

"Yeah, I guess I do. It's my home."

"The department doesn't pay you enough to rent an apartment or buy a house?" Helen asked.

"Yeah, my salary covers that. But my ex-wife and two kids live in it. After I pay child support, alimony, and utilities, I barely have enough to live on. I sold my Kawasaki motorcycle and got just enough to buy that van and get it inspected and licensed. If it weren't for the van, I'd be totally homeless."

"You don't look like no homeless person, Jeremy," Helen said pointedly.

"I shower and shave at Planet Fitness. Costs me ten dollars per month. Figure I can afford that luxury. My kind of work just requires jeans and tee shirts. I get the jeans for twelve dollars new at Walmart. I get by, but life was better when I was married."

"Not too many men would admit to that," Helen

said.

"So, what about Squiggles?" I asked. "Can you bring her in so we can ask her a few questions? We tried to find your truck the other day, but you moved it on us. Didn't know it was you, or we would have come directly to you."

"Gonna pick her up at Walmart at six. She works there part-time. Want to follow me? Maybe you guys could interview her at Salad Sammy's and maybe you'd spring for our dinners? It's our five-month anniversary and I'd love to do something special for her."

"Sure," Helen said. "Anything for young lovers."

"We're hardly young, Detective Martin. My kids are in high school."

****

At six-fifteen, Helen and I met Jeremy and Squiggles at Salad Sammy's, a place on the border of Marshfield and Willow Falls with a fifty-foot-long salad bar. As we were being seated by the hostess, I learned that an "all you can eat" salad bar experience cost only twelve dollars, including drink and dessert. Alcoholic beverages cost extra, so Squiggles and Jeremy ordered three cocktails apiece to celebrate their anniversary. I quickly calculated six drinks at eight dollars apiece equaled four extra salad bar experiences. Justifying it on my expense account would be dicey.

Jeremy introduced Helen and me as work associates. Squiggles shook both our hands, and then suggested that the line at the salad bar seemed short enough to accommodate everybody. After piling our plates with a variety of vegetable delights, Helen and I joined Jeremy and his girlfriend at their table. The hostess soon delivered the six cocktails. Helen had opted for lemonade from a three-gallon serve-yourself station, and I had opted for a sixteen ounce no-name cola of some kind from a machine nearby.

"How did you two meet?" Squiggles asked when we had begun eating.

"Oh, we're not a couple," I replied. "We work together, that's all."

Squiggles did not know she was the subject of an interview. "Actually," Helen said, "we asked Jeremy if he'd introduce us to you because we're hoping you can help us on a case we're investigating."

Squiggles shot a disappointed look at her boyfriend. "I thought you said this was an anniversary dinner."

"And Jeremy thought he was the only person to call you 'Squiggles,' Kameesha," I said. "That makes you about even."

Squiggles shot Jeremy a dirty look and threw her napkin on the table. "Take me home, Jeremy."

"Home is right outside, Kameesha," I said. "We know you live in the van with Jeremy."

"Squiggles," Jeremy pleaded gently, "if you would, please listen to Helen and Bart and answer the few questions they have. It would mean a lot to me."

Kameesha folded her arms and rolled her eyes. "I got no place to go anyway. Go ahead…"

"We're looking into the death of the guy they called Big Wax," Helen said. "I understand you were there when he was buried."

Kameesha inhaled deeply and then exhaled forcefully from her mouth. "Yeah, it was me and three other girls what found him in the garage. Jasmine stood guard outside and me and the other two dug a hole and rolled him into it. There ain't much else to tell."

"What about the leather jacket?" I asked, taking a bite of potato salad.

"That was Darla's. She took it off and throwed it over his face before we shoveled dirt onto him."

"And was he missing any fingers?" I asked.

Kameesha swallowed a mouthful of pickled beets. "I didn't look at nothing like that."

"What about his ring?" Helen asked, putting a forkful of egg salad into her mouth.

"That big old thing?" Kameesha replied. "He used to wave that thing at Jasmine and get her all upset. He sometimes hit me and the other girls with it. When he did, it had a sharp edge that would cut our skin. He was a nasty bastard, you know." Kameesha ate a forkful of three bean salad.

Helen nodded. "We've heard that." She stuffed another bite of egg salad into her mouth.

I got to the point. "Jasmine wears a ring with a square black stone around her neck. It's on a silver chain. Is that Big Wax's ring?"

Kameesha put down her fork. "You know, I never gived it much thought, but I think it is. Yes, it is! Same black stone, same silver color. I believe it is. Is that important?"

Jeremy swallowed his mouthful of chicken salad. As he did, he patted Kameesha on her forearm. "Yes, honey, I think so. You know the skeleton I told you about? The one from a couple of weeks ago?"

"Yes?"

"It was missing its pinkie finger. We never found it."

"That's the finger Big Wax wore his ring on. His

right hand?"

Jeremy nodded. "Yes, right."

Helen gave Jeremy a serious look. "You shouldn't be discussing the details of any case with anybody, not even your best friend or your spouse. It could compromise our investigation."

"I know, and I'm sorry. But I did tell Squiggles about that case. I was proud we found the entire skeleton. Well, except for the little finger and a leg bone. I guess I broke protocol, huh?"

"We won't report you this time because you introduced us to Squiggles," I said. "Just be sure to follow the rules next time."

"How long ago did Big Wax take the ring from Jasmine?" Helen asked.

"We was teenagers. I'd say she was sixteen or seventeen. No way to know for sure."

"How long has Jasmine been wearing that necklace with the ring around her neck?" I asked.

"About four…." She wiped her lips with her paper napkin. "Are you saying Jasmine killed Big Wax? Just to get her ring back?"

"No, we're not saying anything," I replied. "We're still trying to figure out how he died…and maybe why he died. We don't think any of you four girls killed him." I wiped my mouth with a brown paper napkin. "Back to my question. When did Jasmine begin wearing the ring around her neck again?"

"'Bout since the time Big Wax disappeared."

Helen finished her plate and went to get dessert. She had to choose between vanilla tapioca or macaroons. She put a little of both on a small plate and returned to the table.

"I thought you were getting seconds," I said, looking at her meager dessert.

"I eat any more and I'll have to buy a larger girdle."

Kameesha giggled. "You two are funny."

"Remember what we told Jeremy, Kameesha?" I asked. "Same thing goes with what we've talked about tonight. You can't tell anybody what we've talked about. Not even Darla, Jasmine, or Nadine. Understand?"

"Especially not them," Helen emphasized.

Kameesha nodded. "I promise."

"She'll do things the right way. I know my girl," Jeremy said putting his arm around her and pulling her close. He kissed her in front of us. "I love you, honey."

Helen looked at me. "Isn't that sweet? Five months is a long-term relationship in today's world."

Chapter 47

The campaigning in West Virginia came to a close on the tenth of May, and elections were held on the twelfth. It had been a bitterly contested campaign for Michael Agosta. Both he and Audrey had defended his reputation and record against constant and severe mudslinging by the West Virginia Democrats about his personal and professional reputations. Audrey was steadfast during the daily assault by the reporters, but at night she often broke into tears from the onslaught. Michael, in contrast, became angrier and more resolute, especially when the charge of rape was probed by reporter after reporter, each looking for a crack in his responses to their biased questioning.

During the morning of May twelfth, Michael and Audrey were accompanied by their daughter Charlotte to the local polling site, where all three cast their ballots for Michael. After voting, they joined members of the Conservative and Republican parties at Sybil's Diner for a brief breakfast to thank the many supporters who had worked tirelessly on his campaign. Then they headed home to rest until after dinner, when they ventured to the local United Mine Workers Meeting Hall to watch televised results projected onto three large screens—one each for the local affiliates of ABC, NBC, and CBS. At midnight they drove home, somewhat despondent because the race was too close to call. The results would have to wait until the following day.

At ten o'clock in the morning, Ben called. "Is Audrey home, Michael?" he asked.

"Yeah. You want to speak with her?"

"No, I want her to pick up another extension, or else put her on speaker phone."

There was a metallic rustle on the phone. "Okay, Ben we're both on."

Two voices burst into song, "For he's a jolly good fellow…for he's a jolly good fellow…Congratulations, your honor!"

"Did Hamilton concede?" Michael asked.

"Hell, no, Mikey," a second voice said. "He didn't have to. You won by a clean one thousand votes." The voice belonged to Carl. Carl always called him 'Mikey,' especially when he was excited.

"Michael?" Ben asked. "Michael? He didn't pass out, did he?"

"You'll have to forgive me, gentlemen. I was kissing my wife. Over the last six months, she has stood by me through more shit than any wife should have to."

"That's okay, Mikey. If I was there, I'd be kissing her, too."

"Listen, Michael, you and Audrey need to get dressed and meet us down at the UMW Hall at noon," Carl said. "We've got all the campaign workers and the press coming to hear what you have to say. Just thank them. Be humble. And be the best damn Supreme Court of Appeals judge this state has ever seen."

"Hey, there's almost no time to shower and shave. I'd better get hopping."

"Okay Michael, see you there."

"Yeah, Mikey. You done great!"

****

Michael and Audrey stood on the stage at the United Mine Workers Hall, smiling and greeting everyone who waved or shouted at them. Ben spoke to the crowd on behalf of the WV Republican Party, and Muriel Andress, Chairwoman of the State's Conservative Party, spoke on behalf of her membership. Both promised less legislation from the bench and the reversal of decisions which had been purely political at the hand of Michael's predecessor, Penelope Sutch.

It was unusual for a winning candidate to take questions from the press at such events, but Michael broke tradition and recognized a few reporters whose hands were raised. The first, a woman with orange hair asked, "Is it true you and Mrs. Agosta had to get married?"

Audrey froze at the question, but Michael smiled and casually replied, "No, nobody forced us to get married. We entered into Holy Matrimony of our own accord. I am even more in love with my wife now than I was then. Ours was a match made in heaven."

He quickly turned to the opposite side of the stage, where a young man had his hand raised. "Sir," the reporter asked, "it has come to my attention you recently won a large lawsuit against Albany County, New York, for false arrest and character assassination. How much were you able to settle for?"

Michael smiled. "Yes, the trumped-up charge against me was entirely fallacious and the lawsuit was settled in my favor. By law, I am not able to disclose the amount. However, I have divided the award and have contributed it in equal shares to three homes for unwed mothers and to three private adoption agencies that place unwanted children into homes where they will be loved and cared for until long after they are adults."

The crowd cheered and applauded.

Michael risked another question from the woman with orange hair. "How much have you donated to Planned Parenthood?" she asked.

Michael smiled. "Let me be very clear about my posture on abortion. Although as a judge and adjudicator I will uphold constitutional laws permitting abortion, I have not and will not contribute my personal funds to abortion clinics."

Once again, the crowd erupted into cheers and applause. Michael pulled Audrey to him, placed his arm around her waist, and the two of them waved to the crowd for a full five minutes, until Ben came to them and escorted them off the stage.

Chapter 48

At nine o'clock in the morning on May fourteenth a black and white police cruiser parked in front of Jasmine Goins' duplex. Two uniformed officers left the motor running and climbed the stairs to Jasmine's apartment. They handcuffed her, read her the Miranda Rights and then escorted her down the stairs and onto the street. The female officer put her hand onto Jasmine's head to protect it as Jasmine fell onto the cruiser's back seat. When the door closed, Jasmine saw it had no door handle. Even if she could escape the cuffs, there was no escape from the police cruiser.

****

Half an hour later, a different police cruiser pulled up and double parked on the street where Darla Borst lived with her macho, Rolando. When the officers knocked on her door, Rolando answered and then fell backward against his couch when he saw police at his door. "You ain't come for me, has you?" he asked.

"Not unless your name is Darla Borst," the male officer said.

"Darla?" Rolando called out. "You got company."

Darla ambled down the hallway from the bathroom, dressed in her underwear and an oversized white tee shirt. She was expecting Nadine, but not so early.

"Darla Borst?" the female officer asked.

Darla was surprised Nadine had not come. She nodded to the officer.

The officer removed the handcuffs from her belt. "We've come to arrest you on suspicion of murder."

Darla turned and ran down the hallway, hurrying into her bedroom and locking the door. She found her cell phone and called her sister. When Margo answered, Darla screamed, "What you do...turn me in or something? You're a bitch."

Margo hung up the phone. *Darla must be out of her mind.*

A clicking sound came from the bedroom door, and then it opened. "Get dressed, Ms. Borst," the female officer said. "You have an appointment downtown."

She was trapped and there was nothing she could do. So, Darla dressed in comfortable clothes -- an older sweatpants and sweatshirt combo, white socks, and her slippers. The female officer put cuffs on her, read her the Miranda Rights, and escorted her into the living room. She kissed Rolando goodbye and asked him to see what he could do about raising bail. "I didn't do nothing," she said.

He nodded and stared open-mouthed as his live-in woman was escorted away by City police.

Jasmine and Darla arrived at the police department half an hour apart. They were processed separately and placed into interrogation rooms at the opposite ends of the same hallway. Each woman sat in her room for over an hour, handcuffed to a steel table, hungry, and afraid.

Helen and I decided to work on Darla first, Helen playing good cop and I playing bad. Consistent with our roles, Helen wore a soft pink cotton sweater and tan slacks. Her hair was picked into a short Afro accented with large gold hoop earrings. In contrast, I wore my official police uniform, steel gray with dark blue leg stripes. Around my waist was a thick black leather belt with holstered pistol, mace, and handcuffs clearly visible.

I started first. "We meet again, Darla. You lied to us about your role in the death of Harold Waxman, a.k.a. 'Big Wax.' We're prepared to charge you with his murder."

"You got nothing on me," Darla said. "I didn't do nothing."

"Your leather jacket tells us otherwise. We found traces of narcotics, blood, and mucous. And, of course, a name written inside associates the jacket with you. We also have corroborating testimony from the three women who helped you bury Big Wax after you killed him. An all-white jury is going to run with that evidence and send you to prison for life."

"Don't do that. Don't send me to prison. I got children."

"You should have thought about that before you killed Big Wax. But Rolando will take good care of your children, especially your daughter. He might even invite her into his bed since you won't be around to service him."

"You're a sick bastard, Mr. Jones. A real sick bastard."

There was a knock on the door. Helen Martin entered. "Chief wants to see you, Jones. He's got more news about some piece of evidence."

I stood and gave Darla a hard look. "Don't you go anywhere." Then I laughed and exited the room.

Helen sat across from Darla. "You want coffee or

anything?"

"He's different from the way he was last time I saw him," Darla said.

"He's bucking for a promotion. Thinks if he can hang this murder on you, he'll make captain."

"That's not fair. I didn't do nothing."

"Can you give me anything to prove that? Can you prove you didn't kill Big Wax?"

"Course not, Miss. Can you prove you didn't kill him instead of me? No way."

"Well, he's got your jacket and your DNA is on it," Helen lied. "That connects you to the crime scene. Then he's got the testimonies of the other girls, who say you were the leader of the burial activity. Jones figures you killed Big Wax and then brought the others to help bury him. Is he right about all of that?"

Darla's eyes descended. "Big Wax was a mean man, always taking people's stuff. He decided he wanted to be a pimp. He figured me and the other girls would be his whores. We don't want that. But he hit us and forced us to do sex with him and his friends. Said we was 'in training.' We need the Clan to help us live day by day, but we nobody's whores."

"So, are you saying any one of you could have killed him? You just gave a motive for his murder."

"Yeah, I guess I am, but it wasn't me."

"But what about your leather jacket?"

"I was wearing it, not him. We wasn't going steady, not like with the other guys I gave it to when we was going together steady, you know what I mean?"

Helen nodded.

****

Jasmine jumped when I forcefully opened the door

to the interrogation room where she was waiting. Her eyes followed me as I walked in a circle around her and then sat in the chair across the table. I was still playing bad cop, enjoying the role which truly was unnatural for me.

"You're going down," I said. "Murder One."

"What's that mean?"

"Intentional. You planned it and did it. Heartless, premeditated murder. Cold-blooded."

Jasmine's eyes watered and she clenched her fists. "I didn't do nothing like that."

I held up the necklace and ring which had been removed from her neck during the in-take procedure. "This was on Big Wax's finger at the time of his murder. I got witness testimony that it was your ring, and Big Wax took it from you and tormented you with it. He's dead and you've got the ring. You murdered him for the ring."

"I did no such thing, and I want my ring back."

"No way you'll see this ring again. It's evidence of the murder. It's been through DNA analysis this morning," I lied, "and it's got your DNA and Big Wax's DNA on it. That puts both of you together at the time of his death. The all-white jury will hang you for murder."

"That's my ring from my daddy. It never belonged to Big Wax. He took it and made my life miserable about it, but I didn't kill him."

There was a knock on the door and Helen entered. "Chief wants to see you, Jones. He's got more evidence which proves it was murder."

"Stay here, Jasmine. I'll be back in a few minutes with more evidence to hang you."

Jasmine burst into tears.

Helen sat across the table and handed her a tissue. "He's really a good guy, but something's up his butt. He wants to close this case with a murder charge. He thinks he's got you."

"It weren't no murder. Maybe a accident, but no murder."

"Accident? You want to tell me about it? Maybe I can calm him down, reduce the charges."

Jasmine nodded and blew her nose. Helen handed her another tissue. Jasmine took it and started talking like a canary on overdrive.

"Nobody like Big Wax. I hung with him for a couple of months, but we wasn't boyfriend and girlfriend. He was mean to me. Hit me a lot. Took any money and any dope I had on me. He took the ring my father gave me. When we broke up, he kept the ring and showed it to me when he was with other girls, lots of them. Eventually I quit seeing him. I pushed over his precious motorcycle. Big black thing with a windshield. It dent the tank. I had to hide from him, 'cause he put out a contract among the Clan for finding me. What was I going to do? My whole life was them Clan. "

Helen stood and got Jasmine a cup of water from the white plastic water cooler which stood against the concrete wall behind her.

"Thanks," Jasmine said. She took a long swallow, put the paper cup down, and started her story again. "I stayed in the empty house on Spencer Street for a few weeks. My friends, them three other girls, they brought me food and clean clothes and magazines to read."

Helen nodded, indicating she understood and that Jasmine should keep telling her story.

"One night, Big Wax, he found me and took me down to the garage, where two other Clan was waiting. They all raped me. What you call that?"

"Gang rape?"

"Yeah, that's it. Gang rape. They gang-raped me. He told me it was a initiation…he was planning to pimp me out. After they finish their business with me, all three of them, they shot up and fell asleep."

"What did they shoot up?" Helen asked.

"Belushi. You know what that is?"

Helen nodded. It was a concoction of heroin and cocaine, the stuff that killed actor John Belushi.

"I found their dope, cooked a second spoonful of the powder and shot it into Big Wax's vein so he wouldn't wake up when I took my ring off his little finger. He fall deep asleep. But I couldn't get the ring off. It was stuck behind that big knuckle. So, I went back into the house to watch what happen. When the others wake up from their sleep, he didn't wake up. He died from the dope, not from me. They left his body there."

"So, how'd you get your ring back?" Helen asked.

"Next day, I went and got Darla, and me and her went into the garage and cut off his finger to get the ring. Had to bring his finger home and cut it up with a butcher knife to get the ring off. That mean man just wouldn't let go of it. Washed it in vodka and put it on my chain, where it been ever since.

"Next night Darla and me, we get the other girls and go look at the house where Darla's little sister got pregnant. Darla say we all should go out back. When we did, that smell from the garage was awful, worse than rotten meat. Squiggles open the door and Big Wax was lying dead, his eyes wide open looking at the ceiling and his belly big like a pumpkin. Darla send me outside to keep watch, and she and the other two buried him. And just like that it was done."

"So, you're saying Harold Waxman died of a drug overdose and you're not guilty of murdering him, even though you gave him the second injection of Belushi?"

"We never knowed his real name. What you call him? Harold? Everybody just call him "Big Wax.""

****

After conferring with me, Helen went back to see Darla.

Darla was wiggling in her chair when Helen entered the room. "Can I go use the ladies' room?" Darla asked.

"After I'm finished asking you a couple of more questions."

"Well, you better hurry 'cause my body told me to start dancing a couple minutes ago."

"You need to know Jones is busy with the District Attorney, filing an affidavit to charge you with murder. I'm pretty sure you didn't do it, but you got to fess up, girl. Your friend gave you up. Said you killed him and helped her cut off Big Wax's finger."

"She say that? No way she say that."

"Yes, she said that. Now I want to know the truth, and your story had better gel with hers or the only ladies room you'll get to use is the steel pot in your cell."

Darla crossed her legs to keep from wetting her underpants. "Jasmine, she's the one who told, ain't she? Well, Jasmine came and told me Big Wax was doing smack and he dead. You know, he was dead before she came to me. I didn't murder nobody. Jasmine was in a fret. Told me Big Wax had her daddy's ring on his little finger, and she want it back. She said she tried to pull it off, but his finger was all swollen and the ring wouldn't come off. I said, 'we should go and cut his finger off. If he's dead, he won't be needing that finger no more.' So, I got Rolando's pruning shears and Jasmine showed me where the body was, and we cut the ring away."

"Did you cut off the whole finger?"

"Yeah, mostly. We tried to just cut off part of it, but that didn't work, so we cut mostly the whole thing off. We took the finger back to Jasmine's place and used a butcher knife to get her ring off. That was hard work. Took several cuts. I think the ring was always too small for him and he couldn't get it off hisself. That's why he never gave it back to her."

"What did you do with the finger?"

"Jasmine said she just put it out in the garbage."

Helen stood and called the cell guard. "Please take this woman to the ladies' room, and then escort her back here."

"Thank you, Lord." Darla said.

Chapter 49

Helen and I were at Ruby's Red Hots together for the first time in four months. She was enjoying her second "weenie all the way," and I was chomping on my third. Both of us were wearing stone-washed blue jeans and Willow Falls High School Golden Eagles sweatshirts, as if we had planned to look like twins.

"Strange, isn't it, how the Borst sisters were both involved in wrongful deaths," Helen said, "but both got out barely scathed by the legal system."

"Yeah," I replied, "I'm not sure if the disparity in their sentences was fair. Darla only had to pay a small fine for illegal dismemberment of a cadaver. But Margo is still doing many hours of community service for not reporting the death of her stillborn son."

"*If* he really was stillborn and didn't die from exposure."

I nodded. "God only knows, Helen."

"Well, Margo knows, and she'll carry it to her grave." Helen took another bite of her hotdog. "What do you think the court's gonna do about Jasmine?"

I swallowed a mouthful of masticated meat and bun. "It's hard to say. She's been charged with manslaughter and third-degree murder. I'm not sure either charge will stick, especially murder."

"Why's that?" Helen asked, licking meat sauce from her little finger.

"To truly be third degree, the victim's death has to be associated with another felony, and I don't think trying to get your personal property back is considered a felony, especially when it's a ring the deceased stole and you can't get it to slide off his finger."

Helen nodded and took a sip of her cola.

"Big Wax was an undesirable character," I continued, "and I think the D.A. is just as happy to see him in the ground as the three women are. He's no loss to humanity."

"And when the jury hears Jasmine's story," Helen said, "they're probably going to feel sympathy for her. She's had a tough life and she's not well-educated. She was probably doing the only thing she could think of to get justice for Big Wax's theft of her property."

I crumpled my napkin and plopped it on my plate.

Helen followed suit. "It's been nice working with you on this case, Jonesy. We'll have to work together again sometime. I'm feeling kind of close to you now. When you gonna leave that wife of yours and take up with me?"

"Maybe this afternoon after I call Jasmine's attorney. Her trial begins next week."

"The Court-appointed guy?"

"Yeah. I think I'm going to ask him to call me to the witness stand to support a light sentence, maybe exoneration. I don't think Jasmine deserves to do any hard time."

"When you done talking with him, come spend time with me, you hear? I'll make it worth your while…maybe take you to eat in a fancy restaurant. I know a good fish place."

I smiled. "Sure."

A word about the author…

Born in Massachusetts, Edward Baker traveled widely as a child because his U.S. Marine father was transferred on a regular basis to new assignments across the U.S.A. By the time Ed was twelve, he had crossed the United States three times. And as a licensed driver at the ripe old age of sixteen, he drove a stick shift Ford across the nation, following his dad, who was pulling a camping trailer behind the family's station wagon.

An English major at Elon College, Ed earned a master's degree at Appalachian State University and a doctorate in Educational Leadership at the Sage Colleges' Esteves School of Education. After thirty-five years in higher education and after retiring as Interim President of a public community college, he turned his attention to his first love, writing, while continuing to teach undergraduate and graduate courses on an adjunct basis at a private college in upstate New York.

During the cold months, they "hole up" in their winter quarters in Saratoga Springs, New York. However, during the warm months, Ed and his wife reside in their cabin on Galway Lake, New York. When he's not writing or engaged in a woodworking project, Ed can be found on the lake or playing with his grandchildren or his four-legged canine companion Sudsy.

www.edwardsbaker.com

Thank you for purchasing
this publication of The Wild Rose Press, Inc.

For questions or more information
contact us at
info@thewildrosepress.com.

The Wild Rose Press, Inc.
www.thewildrosepress.com

www.ingramcontent.com/pod-product-compliance
Lightning Source LLC
Chambersburg PA
CBHW051537260626

47170CB00003B/974